PROTECTING ELLIOT

A PROTECTORS NOVELLA

SLOANE KENNEDY

Mel—
Happy Reading! ♡

Sloane Kennedy

CONTENTS

Cover Images: © JANIFEST

Cover Design: © Jay Aheer, Simply Defined Art

Copyediting by Courtney Bassett

ISBN-13:
978-1978144996

ISBN-10:
1978144997

PROTECTING ELLIOT

Sloane Kennedy

TRADEMARK ACKNOWLEDGEMENTS

ACKNOWLEDGMENTS

A big thank you to Claudia and Kylee for doing such a quick beta read for me and to Courtney for the fantastic editing job.

AUTHOR NOTE

Although it features several characters from my other books and is part of the "Protectors" world, Protecting Elliot is a stand-alone novella that can serve as a great way to get a feel for the Protectors/Barretti/Finding universe I've created.

In regards to the timeline of events, Protecting Elliot occurs after Book 9 in my Protectors series, but it is not necessary to read any other books to enjoy this novella. I've specifically written this book to give new readers a chance to meet my guys and for loyal fans to check in with old favorites while still meeting a new couple.

For those of you who are new to my books, there is a suggested series reading order and crossover chart (these can also be found on my website) at the end of this novella that will help you determine where to start if you end up enjoying Cruz and Elliot's story. I've also heard from many readers that all my series can be read out of order, so feel free to jump in with any book that catches your eye. Happy reading!

PROLOGUE

Cruz

"Cruz, come on in," Memphis said after shaking my hand. I nodded and followed my boss to the living room. I wasn't surprised to see Ronan waiting there. Despite the man's increasing focus on his family and medical career, he still had his fingers in every aspect of the vigilante group he'd founded.

I'd never personally met the third man in the room, but I knew who he was. Memphis had already given me the heads-up that he was a close friend of his and Ronan's and that he was connected to the powerful Barretti family.

"Cruz, this is Declan Barretti," Memphis said.

"Captain," I said politely as I extended my hand to the man who'd risen from his position on the couch. He tilted his head at me, probably because I'd used his formal title rather than his name.

"Please, call me Declan," he murmured as he shook my hand. I already knew the man was in his late forties, since I'd done as much research on him as I could once Memphis had told me about the meeting. I'd spent the better part of the evening weeding through the murky family tree that was the Barretti clan. Declan had actually married into the family years earlier, though I wasn't sure if marriage was the correct term, since he was in a relationship with two men at the same time. I'd seen some news articles about Declan and his partners, Ren Barretti and Jagger Varos, having had some type of commitment ceremony, but I wasn't about to ask about it.

It certainly wasn't any of my business.

I was here to do a job, nothing more.

"Declan," I said with a nod.

I stepped past Declan and shook Ronan's hand, then took the chair that Ronan motioned to. It was a good spot because it would allow me to read Declan's expressions as he spoke. Despite the fact that he was close to Ronan and Memphis, I still wanted the ability to judge for myself how forthcoming the man was.

Declan was a big guy and a good-looking one, but there was a certain weariness about him. I wondered if it had anything to do with why I'd been called in. The fact that he was a captain in the Seattle Police Department had piqued my interest from the get-go, since it wasn't typical for a do-it-by-the-books cop to seek the help of guys like Ronan and Memphis.

After all, it wasn't like what me and the other guys who worked for Ronan did was exactly aboveboard.

"Declan has asked us for assistance with a case," Memphis began before deferring to Declan.

Declan swallowed hard and nodded. I had to wonder if whoever the subject was had some kind of personal connection to Declan because he seemed pained as he tried to figure out where to start.

"His name is Elliot Wittier," Declan said. Memphis handed me a file folder and I quickly flipped it open. My eyes fell on the picture that was on top of the stack of papers. I quelled my reaction to the sight of the gorgeous man and promptly shut the folder again.

I'd have time to study the contents later. For now, I wanted to focus all my attention on the man asking for my help.

But the piercing blue eyes, dirty blond hair, and rangy body from the photograph rode the edge of my vision as Declan began speaking.

"We received a 911 call last night from the office of the foundation he runs. Elliot was returning to the office to pick up something on his way home from a dinner meeting. He walked in on someone vandalizing the place and got roughed up."

My fists automatically tightened on the folder in my hands. "Is he okay?" I asked quickly, despite my intent to remain emotionally detached from the police captain's story.

"Couple of scrapes and bruises. He declined medical treatment."

I nodded and ignored the need to fire more questions at Declan.

I also ignored the innate desire to flip the folder open again so I could take in Elliot's image once more. Even now, I was wondering about the severity of his injuries.

It wasn't a good sign.

"When I heard about the attack, I went down there myself," Declan said.

"You have a personal connection to him?" I asked.

Declan paused and shifted his eyes to the ground briefly. "I do," he said softly. I was surprised when Ronan settled his hand on Declan's shoulder.

"There's no judgement here, Declan," Ronan said gently.

Declan nodded. "Elliot is the son of the man I was partnered with shortly after I got out of the police academy. His name was Mac. I wasn't out back then, but Mac was. The department wasn't exactly tolerant when it came to homosexuals on the force. Mac, he didn't care, but I did. I knew what it meant."

When Declan seemed too pained to continue, I said, "Your brothers in blue wouldn't have your back."

Declan nodded and then he was looking directly at me. "Ronan said you'd get it."

I swallowed hard at that.

I got it all too well.

And that fact made it clear as to why I'd been chosen for this particular job.

SLOANE KENNEDY

I managed a nod in response, but nothing else.

"I asked to be assigned to a new partner. My request was granted," Declan continued. "When I next saw Mac, he'd been notified of the transfer and he..."

Declan's words fell off, but neither Ronan nor Memphis urged him to go on. It was a good thirty seconds before he did.

"He told me he understood and that he thought I was going to make a hell of a good cop. He was killed that night responding to a home invasion. His backup never showed up."

Declan took in a shuddering breath before he said, "No one in the department was ever disciplined for it. The higher-ups bought the story that the units who should have responded misunderstood the address dispatch gave them. The fuckers were joking about it the next day – said the best kind of..."

Declan covered his mouth with his hand briefly, then forced the ugly words out. "The best kind of fag was a dead one." The older man paused, then explained, "I was one of two people who went to the funeral. The other was Mac's boyfriend, Sam. Turned out that Mac's family had disowned him. Sam didn't know who I was at first, but afterward when he found out..."

Declan's voice dropped off and this time, he didn't continue.

"Mac had a son?" I finally prodded.

He nodded. "I didn't even know they were expecting. Elliot was born via surrogate a month later. Mac never even got to meet him."

It took Declan several long beats before he seemed to collect himself. "Sam was only a few years older than me when Mac died. He'd started a successful investment firm and just recently handed the reins over to Elliot. But from everything I've seen and heard, Elliot's true passion is the foundation."

It didn't surprise me one bit that Declan had apparently been keeping tabs on Mac's child. "What kind of foundation is it?" I asked.

"It focuses on the rights of LGBTQ individuals by providing legal support in discrimination and court cases. It also donates money to different causes and educates the community."

4

I nodded in understanding. It was no surprise that the young man and his foundation would have been targeted. The support for same-sex relationships had grown in leaps and bounds over the years, but it was far from perfect.

"So, you think someone is targeting Elliot?" I asked, suddenly eager to get started on my assignment. Even the idea that danger could be stalking Elliot Wittier at this very moment was making me antsy.

"It's not the first time the place has been vandalized, but I think it's the first time he's been directly attacked. I don't think he wanted me to know it, but he seemed really spooked by the whole thing. But when I offered to beef up patrols in the neighborhood, he told me not to bother." Declan's tone made it clear why Elliot had declined the offer – the young man clearly doubted the cops would take any better care of him than they had his father.

Declan's eyes held mine as he said, "I just need to make sure it was a onetime thing. I owe it to Sam... and Mac."

"Understood," I said. "Why not just put some police protection on him? Or ask your brothers-in-law to have someone watch him?" I asked.

"Elliot shares his father's hatred of all things police. I doubt he would have even reported the incident last night if a passerby hadn't seen what was happening and called 911. When we arrived, he wasn't exactly cooperative... or welcoming. Not that I can really blame him." Declan paused before saying, "I can't ask Dom to put one of his guys on Elliot because they have both a professional and personal relationship."

I knew Dom was Dominic Barretti, Declan's brother-in-law and one of the co-founders of Barretti Security Group. Dom had been married to Declan's younger sister, Sylvie, for several years before losing her to leukemia. He'd gone on to marry a man named Logan Bradshaw, while Declan had become involved with Dom's younger brother, Ren, and one of Dom's employees, Jagger.

"How so?" I asked.

"Sam began contracting with Dom's security group years ago. Barretti Security Group handles Sam and Elliot's investment firm's information technology security needs. Sam didn't know when he signed on with Dom's group that Dom and I were related by marriage. Once he found out, he chose not to dissolve the professional relationship because Barretti Security is just too good at what it does. Dom wasn't sure about keeping Sam's business when he found out how much Sam and his son hated me, but I convinced him to put that aside and keep the relationship."

"And the personal relationship?" I asked.

"Dom's husband, Logan, runs a center that helps LGBTQ kids. It gets them off the streets and provides them with resources like education, housing, counseling, and legal support. Elliot's foundation is a big contributor and he and Logan have become friends."

"That must be awkward," I murmured.

Declan sighed softly. "Just shows what good men Sam and Elliot are. Despite their hatred of me, they're not going to let the people who rely on them suffer. I imagine Elliot and Logan have come to some kind of agreement that the topic of me is off-limits."

Declan shifted forward on the couch a bit and pressed his hands together. "So, you can see why I can't ask Dom to get involved. I just... I need to know the threat to Elliot, if there is one, is taken care of. But he can't know I'm involved—"

"He won't," I cut in. "I'll make sure of it."

Though I didn't have any kind of personal connection with Declan or his huge family, I owed it to Ronan and Memphis to make sure this job didn't go sideways. "I'll find a way to get close to him without him being the wiser," I murmured before glancing at Memphis and Ronan. Both men nodded and I knew that they were trusting me to figure out the best way to get into Elliot's inner circle. I stood and held my hand out to Declan. "I'll keep him safe," I said.

Declan rose, nodded, then took my hand. "For Mac," he whispered.

"For Mac," I agreed, though I knew in my gut that it wasn't just the obligation to the fallen officer that would have me keeping Elliot out of harm's way.

It was a reality I didn't want to deal with, so I tucked the folder under my arm before saying my goodbyes to Ronan and Memphis.

Time to figure out who exactly Elliot Wittier was and how to keep him from meeting his father's fate.

CHAPTER 1

Elliot

"Keep it together, El," I murmured to myself as I stepped into the ballroom. I wiped my sweaty palms on the scratchy surface of my costume and then cursed the fact that I even had to do it in the first place. I allowed myself a few seconds to focus on my breathing, which quelled the anxiety that was threatening to overtake me, then stepped farther into the room. On most days, the breathing technique helped, but the combination of startled looks sent my way and the quiet murmurs that followed as I began weaving my way through the small crowd had my nerves returning tenfold almost instantly.

I'd never been one for social gatherings of any kind, but they were a necessary evil in my line of work. When it came to managing the investment firm my dad had started and that I'd eventually taken over, I had no issue with delegating the public speaking events to the senior officers. But the foundation was different. It was my baby and I wasn't willing to sacrifice it for the sake of my fear of social engagements.

So being the center of attention at a fundraiser such as this one should have been the norm, but between the bruises on my face and the constant need to scan my surroundings to watch for an impending attack, I was on edge more than normal.

As I began greeting the patrons, ignoring their colorful and sometimes downright ridiculous Halloween costumes as I went, my mind drifted to the events of the night before. I hadn't exactly been honest with the police when they'd questioned me about the incident. I'd told them I'd walked in on the vandals, but in reality, they'd followed me into the office, forcing their way inside as soon as I'd opened the door. I'd known as soon as the bigger of the two men had wrapped his fingers around my throat that they hadn't been there to rough me up because they disagreed with my foundation's mission.

It would have been better if they had been.

No, their motivation had been much less complicated than hatred and a hell of a lot more dangerous.

A shiver filtered through my body as I remembered the veiled threat that had been whispered in my ear right after the Good Samaritan's voice had called through the front door that he was calling for help.

You have three days.

I hadn't needed three days. At least not to figure out what they'd been after. They'd made that part pretty clear by casting one last parting shot my way right before a beefy fist had connected with my jaw for the final time.

Stealing from Mr. White was your first mistake, Wittier. Don't make it your last.

Two days.

I had two days left to figure out how to fix the clusterfuck I'd been thrust into. And I had to do it while pretending life was trudging along as usual.

Which meant getting through the next few hours. Then I'd be back at my computer trying to track down Mr. White's missing money.

I was so busy mentally planning my next steps that I wasn't paying attention to where I was going. When my body ran right into a hard wall, I let out an "oomph" at the same time the wall grabbed a hold of me.

Okay, so not a wall.

My already dry mouth went drier as I took in the man I was currently pressed up against in what would have been considered an intimate embrace in any other situation.

"You okay?" came the deep voice that held just the slightest rasp to it. The strong fingers that were currently wrapped around my upper arms burned right through the thin material of my costume and threatened to singe my skin. Pulse after pulse of energy flared up and down my arms.

"Uh, yeah," I said. "Sorry," I mumbled as I let my eyes rake over him. He was about my height and age, but that was pretty much where the similarities between us ended. Even within the folds of his costume, I could tell he had a ripped body.

Hell, I was practically still pressed up against it, so there was no doubting that the ridges I was feeling were miles and miles of well-defined muscles. His dark-as-night eyes matched the coal black of his hair. A slight five-o'clock shadow hugged the sharp lines of his jaw and I had the sudden urge to feel that stubble all over my body.

"No problem," he said, a slight smile spreading across his beautiful mouth. God, even his teeth were perfect.

I knew I needed to step back, but even as I leaned back a little, he seemed reluctant to release me and I found myself unable to follow through on the move. The ballroom had disappeared completely, as had the dozens and dozens of partygoers. There were no hot lights raining down on me, no fear of the behemoth from the night before showing up to finish what he'd started, no worries about the speech I was expected to make tonight thanking people for donating so generously.

It was just me and the painfully beautiful man holding me.

And the warmth that was filtering through my body.

I was dimly aware of the man talking, but I couldn't make sense of what he was saying. What the hell was wrong with me? It wasn't until I felt the gentle press of fingers into my upper arms that I realized he was rubbing circles into my skin. Even as I cursed the fact that I couldn't feel his actual touch, I jolted back to awareness.

"I'm sorry, what?" I asked dumbly.

Jesus, I needed to get it together.

The man chuckled slightly and the sound went straight to my long-neglected dick.

"I said, 'Nothing is True; Everything is Permitted.'"

The familiar motto brought a shimmer of reality back and I fought off the fog of confusion. It was only when my eyes skimmed his entire body again that his statement made sense.

I laughed.

And fuck if it didn't feel amazing.

"Aguilar," I said with a smile as I took in his costume.

"Ezio," the man said in all seriousness, as if we really were members of the secret brotherhood of assassins from my favorite video game series, Assassin's Creed.

I knew I needed to say something else, but I couldn't stop staring at him.

The feeling seemed to be mutual, because his eyes never left mine. Not even when he released one of my arms to carefully push my hood off. His fingers skimmed my unbruised cheek slightly as he lowered his hand again.

Back to my arm.

Thank God for that.

Fuck, what the hell was wrong with me? Why couldn't I move? Why was it so damn hard to breathe? Why did my body feel like it was going to go up in flames?

"Elliot?"

It wasn't until the man finally stepped back just a little bit that I realized he hadn't been the one to say my name. Why would he? He didn't even know my name.

"Elliot."

"Yeah?" I said absentmindedly as I held onto the other man's gaze. At some point his hands had slid down until they were encircling my wrists.

"Elliot."

It was the humor in the voice that finally got through to me, and I tore my eyes from the man standing just inches from me and turned to see my friend, Logan, and his husband watching me with amusement.

"What?" I asked as the haze of lust began to ease. "What?" I said more loudly as I tugged my hands free of the man's warm hold.

"Hi," Logan said with a knowing smile. If I hadn't been so embarrassed, I would have laughed at the costumes he and his burly husband, Dom, were wearing.

Popeye and Olive Oyl.

Only Logan was dressed as Popeye and his hulking, bald husband was Olive Oyl.

"Um, hi," I stammered. "Hi."

Logan chuckled, as did his husband. "Hi," he repeated. "Looks like a great turnout tonight."

"Yeah," I said. It was only then that I realized that the man and I hadn't been lost in our own little world in some remote corner of the ballroom. No, we'd been smack-dab in the middle of it, surrounded by chattering partygoers and the benefactors I did business with every day.

"Great costumes," Logan said as he motioned between me and the other man. "They're from that video game, right? Did you guys plan this?"

"No!" I blurted out. "I mean, yes... no... fuck." I could feel the heat suffusing my cheeks as all three men stared at me with open humor. I shook my head and blew out my breath. "Yes, they're from Assassin's Creed, but no, we didn't plan this. We just met," I said lamely as I looked at the dark-haired man whose eyes held mine.

"It was a happy coincidence," he said softly, right before he sent me a sexy little wink.

Oh God, the things that wink inspired. "Yeah," I agreed, though I wasn't sure what I was even agreeing to.

I really needed to get a grip. "You guys look great," I managed to say as I forced my attention back to Logan. It was always a weird thing to be around the other man. As much as I liked him and for as long as we'd been working together, there was always the elephant in the room that neither of us ever addressed. It was just one of those things that had *been* as soon as I'd forced myself to overlook the connection between the Sylvie Barretti Hope for Life Foundation director and a certain police officer who'd been playing a part in my life from almost the moment I'd been born.

Thoughts of Declan Barretti threatened to sour my mood, so I forced myself to reach out and shake hands with Dom. In my line of work, I spent more time interacting with Logan than I did his husband, but I'd managed to also forge a relationship with Declan's brother-in-law that was based on mutual respect. Barretti Security Group had been protecting the information of my dad's and my investment firm clients for a long time now, and I had no doubt that Dom Barretti had been tempted at some point to end that relationship in deference to siding with his brother-in-law. But for whatever reason, he hadn't done it and like with Logan, my dad and I had managed to navigate the murky waters of the relationship, though admittedly, it was hard to sidestep the minefield of family relations when it came to such a huge family like the Barrettis and their ties to the community.

"I lost a bet," Dom murmured before he tucked his husband up against his side and pressed a kiss to his temple. "Not that I'm complaining," he added, his voice going husky. A heated look flared between the two men and I had to work really hard to temper the envy that went through me. What would it be like to have someone look at me like that? To have them say something to me and mean something else entirely – something that only he and I would understand?

Logan's hand settled on his husband's stomach as they stared at each other for a moment, then he shifted his attention back to me. "We, ah, heard about what happened last night," Logan said softly as his eyes landed on my face. "Do you need anything?"

I knew what he was really asking and I'd been expecting it. The foundation had been targeted with random acts of vandalism a few times and each time Logan had found out, he'd offered to talk to Dom about beefing up the security for the office.

"Cost of doing business," I said. "You know that."

Logan nodded sadly.

"I could have someone watch the place for a bit till things settle down," Dom offered. "No charge," he added hopefully.

Although part of me was scared enough to actually want to consider the offer, my attacker the night before had made it pretty clear what would happen if they got even a hint that someone was poking around in their business.

No, I was on my own.

"Thank you, but that will just give them what they want," I lied. "They want me to be running scared."

It was a true enough statement since plenty of homophobes had tried to shut me down by scaring me into submission; it just didn't happen to be the case this time around.

Dom frowned, but didn't comment.

Logan let his fingers twine through his husband's as he said, "Well, we wanted to wish you luck on your speech – you're going to do great."

Logan was one of the few people who'd figured out what a fraud I was when it came to public speaking. I put on a good show, but he knew how wrecked I got standing in front of so many people, their undivided attention on me. Even the thought of it had my breathing ticking up again.

"Thanks," I managed to get out.

"Okay, we'll let you get back to it," Logan said. "It was nice to meet you," he added, his eyes on the man standing silently across from me.

At Logan's unspoken question, the man reached out his hand and said, "Cruz. Cruz de la Vega."

"Nice to meet you, Cruz," Logan said with a nod, then Dom was shaking his hand. I barely noticed the couple wandering off to mingle with others because Cruz's eyes were back on me.

"Well, I should go say my hellos to the other guests," I said. "It was really nice to meet you."

I took a step back, but before I could turn away, Cruz was stepping into my space. "We didn't. Not really."

"Didn't what?" I managed to ask, though having the man once again just inches from me was making it so damn hard to breathe again.

"Meet."

"Oh," I said dumbly. "I'm, uh, Elliot. Elliot Wittier." I put out my hand and it was immediately engulfed in a strong, warm grip that I felt all over my body. I'd been attracted to my fair share of guys over the years, but even the best sex I'd ever had couldn't compare to what this man was able to do to me with the simplest of touches. I both wanted to investigate it further and run as far from it as I could.

"Elliot," Cruz murmured.

That was it. Just my name. No "Nice to meet you." No "Pleasure's mine."

No formalities whatsoever.

Just my name spoken in such a way that I was pretty sure he'd found an untapped erogenous zone.

"Cruz," I said. I'd said his name so I could test how it sounded, but it came out more like a breathless plea.

And I wasn't the only one who'd heard it.

Cruz's eyes went impossibly dark and his mouth parted just a little. Then suddenly, his fingers were tightening around mine and he was turning away from me.

But not to walk away.

No, nothing like that.

To steal me away.

And I went willingly.

Hell, I would have likely kneed anyone in the privates if they'd tried to stop us.

Cruz's strong fingers threaded through mine as we weaved through the crowd. It wasn't until we broke free of the warm bodies that I realized where he was taking me.

And I wanted to scream my thanks to the heavens.

There was next to no foot traffic near the alcove he practically dragged me into. A huge potted plant covered in dancing orange and white lights hid our bodies from view as he pressed me back against the wall. His body was flush with mine and there was just no missing what the folds of his costume were able to hide.

Just like the folds of my costume hid mine.

I groaned when his hardness brushed mine and I automatically put my hands on his waist.

To stop him from pulling away?

To keep myself upright?

I wasn't sure and I honestly didn't care. I cared about absolutely nothing in that moment except getting his mouth on mine.

But he didn't kiss me. Instead, his fingers came up to touch the bruise on my jaw, then the one on my cheek. It wasn't until his thumb gently toyed with the marred flesh of my throat where my attacker had held me in his merciless grip that I let out an almost obscene whimper. Twenty-four hours ago, I'd been in this same position and I'd been scared out of my mind at what would happen when those beefy fingers wrapped around my throat. Now all I wanted was Cruz's strong hand encircling that same spot.

It made no sense whatsoever.

"Please," I whispered.

I had no clue what the hell was wrong with me, but I knew the thing that would fix it was in this man's possession. He would know what to do. He would know what I needed.

I closed my eyes when his fingers gently closed around my throat. The pressure that he applied was only enough that I could feel it, not fear it.

And just like that, the anxiety slid from my body like a hot, heavy blanket I'd been carrying around my entire life and had been waiting until this very moment to shed.

It was insanity.

And I never wanted it to end.

But of course, it had to.

All dreams did.

CHAPTER 2

Cruz

I was barely keeping it together and I had no clue how I was managing it.

Because between Elliot's hot, lithe body practically rubbing against mine, his lust-filled eyes glazing over the more I held him in place against the wall, and the breathy whimpers that were falling from his supple lips as I toyed with how much pressure I applied to his throat, I was ready to turn him around and fuck him right then and there. It was only the reddened skin of his throat and the slightly darker oval spots just below his jaw that kept my lust in check.

The fucker had held him like this.

But not to bring him pleasure.

Never in a million years would I have guessed that someone like Elliot Wittier was so naturally submissive. I doubted even he knew what his body was craving.

On paper, the man was the epitome of success. Undergrad and graduate degrees from Ivy League schools, loads of cash in the bank, and a list of personal and professional accomplishments a mile long. Despite the anxiety I'd gotten a glimpse of tonight, he carried himself with an air of confidence and authority. But whatever masks he wore in public, they were falling by the wayside the longer I spent in his presence.

And *his* mask wasn't the only one that was slipping.

We were as different as night and day, but at this moment, I was more in tune with him then I'd ever been with another living soul.

And that was a serious fucking problem.

Yeah, I'd orchestrated running into him and used our mutual costumes to jump-start a conversation, but somehow, we'd shot right past formalities and were working our way to ending up wrapped around each other in a tangle of hot, sweaty, sexually-sated bodies.

Fuck, I just wanted one taste. I was already leaning in when I managed to catch myself. I forced enough space between our bodies to keep from rubbing my cock against his. I let my mouth settle next to Elliot's ear and couldn't help but nip at the soft skin just behind it before whispering, "Who hurt you, Elliot?"

For someone lost in a haze of passion, he recovered quickly because he stiffened at my words. I wasn't ready for the loss, so I shamelessly pressed my body against his and then licked the shell of his ear. I still had my hand around his throat, so I could feel his pulse hammering just beneath his skin. One of the hands he had at my waist slid up my back and threaded through my hair. He was clearly enjoying my ministrations because he cocked his head to the side in invitation. I gave him what he wanted and gently played with the skin behind his ear, then beneath it, before trailing my lips over his jawline. He let out a breathy moan as I lifted my mouth, but when I didn't kiss him like he so obviously wanted, he opened his eyes.

"Who hurt you, Elliot?" I asked again.

This time when he tensed up, I was prepared and I tightened my hold on his throat. Not enough to hurt him, but to show him I was in control.

And that for once, he didn't need to be.

But even though I owned his body in that moment, his mind was still fighting me and he finally shook his head. "No one. I'm fine, really."

The tremor in his voice said otherwise, but I knew I'd lose him if I pressed him too hard. I had to get back to the original objective.

"Do you want to get out of here?" I asked suggestively.

I knew what his answer would be, but I'd planted the question for a reason. I wasn't exactly proud of what I was doing, but I wasn't exactly lying about it, either.

I really did want to get out of there with him.

"I... I can't. I have to mingle. I have this speech..."

"After," I suggested as I began rubbing my thumb over his pulse, which had slowed only slightly.

"I shouldn't," he murmured half-heartedly.

I knew it would be easy to convince him with something as simple as a kiss.

But nothing about kissing Elliot would be simple.

I knew it in my bones.

And I knew the first time that I kissed him, it wouldn't be like this... here. It wouldn't be about rushing through the inherent perfection of tasting him just to get him to agree to something. It would happen when there was no risk of losing him to his obligations and when I wouldn't have to be aware of our surroundings.

I would only have to be aware of him and what he needed from me.

And what he could and would give me in return.

"After," I repeated, my voice firm.

Elliot finally managed a nod and I once again put some space between us. I heard a woman's voice come over the PA system, but I doubted Elliot even noticed because his fingers were playing with the hair at the nape of my neck. It felt so good that I was once again tempted to just drag him out of there, fundraiser be damned.

And I knew he'd follow.

I put my mouth next to his ear again and said, "They're calling you." It took him a good ten seconds to make sense of my words.

"Shit," he said as he scrambled to move away from me. The anxiety slid over him like a familiar cloak and I hated it. So I didn't hesitate to tighten my hold on his throat and pin him against the wall until he stilled.

Fortunately, there was no fear in his eyes as he focused them on me.

"Talk to me," I said firmly. At his questioning look, I glanced over my shoulder at the ballroom and explained, "When you're up there, you find me and you talk only to me. Do you understand me? No one else."

I wasn't sure if he was reacting to the possessiveness in my voice or the permission I was giving him to escape the pressure of having to deal with the sea of faces that would all be focused on him, but it didn't really matter. I'd accomplished what I'd set out to do because he relaxed, then nodded.

"Good," I said. "When you're finished, you and I are leaving. You can tell people you aren't feeling well. I don't care where we go, just as long as it's you and me. *Just* you and me."

I knew I was being high-handed, but I'd seen enough to suspect that was exactly what Elliot needed tonight. I doubted it was something he was looking for twenty-four-seven and I had absolutely no desire for a relationship built on that particular dynamic, but I'd give him whatever he needed to get him through tonight.

So I could meet the real Elliot.

The one I'd only gotten glimpses of so far.

I stepped away from him and immediately hated the loss of contact as I dropped my hand from his throat. So instead, I wrapped my fingers around his and, not caring who was watching, led him past the crowd toward the front of the ballroom where there was a small stage and a single microphone. Once we reached it, a young woman dressed as a strawberry darted onto the stage and announced him. I gave Elliot's fingers a gentle squeeze before I let him go. His eyes held mine for a moment and I felt a measure of satisfaction at how clear and calm they looked.

During my research earlier in the afternoon, I'd found a couple of YouTube videos for speeches he'd done at local events and while to most he'd likely seemed composed, I'd been able to see the uncertainty in his stance and I'd heard the unevenness in his voice. As he stepped onto the stage, I saw a confident young man and when he began speaking, there was only the slightest hint of self-doubt. But as soon as his eyes searched me out and stayed on me, his voice evened out. He was poised enough to subconsciously keep looking back at the rest of the crowd, but I could tell he wasn't seeing them and he was quick to return his eyes to me.

Yeah, he was definitely only seeing me.

I was arrogantly pleased by that, even though I knew I probably shouldn't be. I hadn't ever been in an actual relationship before, so I'd never felt any kind of moment where it seemed like you were the sole focus of someone else's world.

Elliot was giving that to me.

I knew it wasn't real, but I didn't care.

I'd take what I could get.

Because even if I'd wanted it to be real, it couldn't be.

And wasn't that just a fucking shame?

~

*E*lliot's anxiety had returned the moment he'd stepped off the stage and approached me and it was growing worse and worse with every moment he spent in my presence. He'd hidden it well as we'd matriculated through the crowd so he could mingle for a bit and give his excuses for needing to leave early, but the second I'd taken his hand to lead him from the building, he'd gone rigid with tension. If I hadn't known better, I would have thought he was afraid of me, and if his eyes had been darting around us as we walked, I would have attributed his nerves to the attack he'd endured the night before. But his gaze was practically glued to the ground as we walked.

"You okay?" I asked as I gave his hand a little tug to get his attention.

"What? Oh, um, yeah," he said. His eyes met mine only briefly before falling again. We'd left the hotel where the party had been held a few minutes earlier and were making our way down to the waterfront to check out the marketplace and pier. Although it was dark out, the weather was mild and dry, so we'd decided to walk. The streets around us were busy with foot and car traffic. Since it was the night before Halloween, a large number of people were dressed in costumes like us.

Not satisfied with Elliot's response, I tugged him into the doorway of a small shop. The shop itself was closed, but there was enough light from the street lamp and the single row of lights the shop owner had left on to see Elliot's expression as I forced him back against the wall. Thankfully, the spot afforded us a little bit of privacy.

"Try again," I ordered gently as I crowded my way into Elliot's space. He showed no sign of being afraid of me, so I lifted my hands and settled them on his waist. I cursed the fabric of his costume, because there was just no easy way to get my fingers beneath the material to test the softness of his skin.

"I don't do this," he finally said.

"Do what?"

"Leave parties with strangers. Do whatever it is we're going to do."

I smiled at that. "What is it you think we're going to do?" I asked.

I could see a hint of color flood his skin. "Noth…nothing," he said quickly. "I just…"

God, he was adorable when he got all flustered. I lifted one hand and settled it on the wall next to his head. The move had me caging him in even more and I wasn't surprised when it actually relaxed him rather than made him more tense.

"This," he whispered as he drew in a deep breath. "I don't do this."

I knew what he was talking about and was actually surprised he'd had the guts to bring it up.

"I don't let guys put their hand on my throat and like it so damn much that I think I must be going crazy," he murmured. "I don't let them pin me against walls and wish for more. I don't let them tell me what to do or that I'm leaving with them or to only talk to them while I'm giving a speech."

"Are you ashamed of it?" I asked as I lifted my free hand and began

23

skimming my fingers from his jawline, down his throat, to his collarbone.

"I don't even know what *it* is," he whispered, his voice strangled.

And that was the crux of it. I'd already guessed as much, but Elliot was the kind of guy who planned for everything. For all I knew, he was a complete and utter control freak.

Which wasn't a bad thing, since it was an attribute that would serve someone like him well in his professional life. After all, he'd taken over the reins of a hugely successful business at a very young age and he'd taken it a step further and started an organization that would benefit others. An organization that I highly suspected was a tribute to his late father.

"It's okay to let go sometimes, Elliot. To let someone else shoulder the burden," I said softly. "Whether it's for a few minutes, a few hours, or even a lifetime – it doesn't make you weak. It doesn't mean you failed."

"You're not someone," he returned. "I don't know you. The things I let you do back there," – his eyes shifted back in the direction of the hotel – "the things I still want to let you do to me... it's wrong. It's not who I am."

I ignored my body's response to his comment about the things he wanted me to do to him and pulled back just enough to give him some breathing room, since I wanted to make sure he really heard what I had to say.

"First off, giving control over to someone else isn't wrong if it's something you choose to do... if it's something you need. If it's something the person you're giving it to respects and honors. It takes more strength to give control than to keep it. And I don't pretend to understand what this thing is between us, but you giving me that kind of gift – that trust – hell yeah, I'm taking it. Every. Single. Time. And not because I'm some Neanderthal caveman who has to dominate his guy, but because I know just how hard it was for you to do it. And how badly you needed to do it."

I saw Elliot's eyes widen when I indirectly referred to him as my guy, but managed to ignore the need to show him that that was exactly what I was coming to think of him as.

Because it wasn't possible.

Not in the short time we'd spent together.

And more importantly, because I was a fucking fraud. Even if what had gone down in that alcove had had nothing to do with my job, it wouldn't matter to Elliot if he discovered the truth.

God, I'd really fucked this up.

And I was going to keep fucking it up because even after all of that, I still couldn't let him go. I couldn't take the step back that I needed to in order to keep some distance between us, both literal and metaphorical.

"As for the not knowing me part, we're about to fix that. Because believe it or not, right now, as badly as I want to fuck you until neither of us can move, I want the answer to a question more."

"What... what question?"

I leaned forward until my lips were by his ear. Predictably, his breathing spiked at the close contact. "Who are you, Elliot Wittier, and what do I have to do to keep you?" I pulled back and said, "If that's something you don't want to answer, then tell me now—"

"I do," he cut in. "I have no idea why, but I do."

It was ridiculous how relieved I felt. "Good," I murmured. "Now, let's deal with the last thing that's going to keep you from relaxing." My eyes automatically fell to his mouth as I said, "I'm not going to kiss you tonight."

I swore I heard a little whimper bubble up from his throat, but I couldn't be sure.

"Cruz—" he began, but I put my finger over his lips to silence him, because I knew what he was going to say.

"No," I said firmly. "We're not just going to get it over with." I let my finger test the softness of his bottom lip. "When I taste you for the first time, it's..." I shook my head. "Not fucking rushing it," I finally ground out, because even now, I was fighting the need to lean in and seal my mouth over his.

Instead, I reached down to grab his hand. "Let's go."

I didn't give him a chance to say no, because I knew he didn't want that. And I knew that wouldn't have been his answer, anyway. He was noticeably more relaxed as we made our way down the sidewalk, which pleased me to no end. But my own tension was through the roof when I spotted the familiar figure on the other side of the street. Even in the darkness, I knew what I'd see in those eyes. I knew what question would fall from the lips pulled into a stern frown.

What the hell are you doing, Cruz?

It was a good question. A damn good one.

One I didn't have an answer for and doubted I would anytime soon.

CHAPTER 3

Elliot

ho are you, Elliot Wittier, and what do I have to do to keep you?

It was a question I knew he hadn't really meant, at least not that last part. It had been him getting caught up in the moment, nothing more.

Because shit like this didn't happen in real life.

It was the physical chemistry talking. It was the rush of endorphins from finding someone who had some kind of pull on you that you'd never experienced before. Most, if not all, of what I was feeling was the anticipation – the rush of wondering if it was the real deal, even though deep down I knew it wasn't. Because you didn't meet your other half in a handful of minutes at a Halloween-themed benefit.

Cruz might have liked what he saw in that hotel alcove and again in the doorway of the darkened shop, but it wasn't real. I wasn't that guy. And once he found out who I really was, he'd come up with some excuse to end the evening early and this whole thing would finally be over and I could get back to being boring, uptight, afraid-to-fail Elliot Wittier.

God, why was I even doing this? I needed to be at my computer trying to track down the huge sum of cash that had gone missing from the account of one of the firm's biggest clients.

I was about to turn and tell Cruz that I needed to go, when we reached the doorway of the small diner and he opened the door for me.

He opened the door for me.

Fuck, it really was a date.

A date in which he'd taken sex off the table so I wouldn't have to obsess over it anymore.

Which was what I'd been doing.

Because in addition to all my other less than desirable qualities, I wasn't even a good lay.

"Cruz," I said as I stepped into the diner, but my words died in my throat when he put his hand at the small of my back and steered me in the direction of a booth near the back of the restaurant.

"Yeah?" he said.

I can't do this. I should go.

"I've never been here before. Is it good?" I asked lamely.

Cruz waited until I'd sat down on one side of the booth before he took the other side. Our legs bumped beneath the table, but when I moved mine out of the way, his followed until his calf was pressed up against one of mine. Jesus, he was killing me.

"First thing you need to know about me," Cruz said in lieu of answering the question directly, "is that I love breakfast for dinner. Pancakes, cereal, eggs, doesn't matter. If you offer it to me at the dinner hour, I'm putty in your hands."

I smiled and said, "Duly noted. What should I make you for breakfast?" Cruz's mouth pulled into a little smirk and I felt my cheeks heat. "I mean, not actual breakfast, like, at my place or anything. Just in general... what are your breakfast eating habits in general?"

Breakfast eating habits? Jesus, El, shut the fuck up right fucking now!

Cruz's leg bumped mine under the table and I realized he'd done it to get my attention, because when I looked up from where I'd dropped my eyes to stare at the ugly green Formica tabletop, he sent me what I could only classify as a look of pride.

"I usually work out in the morning, so I typically just have a protein shake. What about you?"

"Oh, well, just coffee. I'm usually out the door pretty early and things are always hectic by the time I get to work."

The waitress appeared. "What'll you boys have?" she asked. She was an older woman with silvery hair that was in some kind of weird updo that lent itself to the whole sixties theme the diner had going on.

Cruz ordered a coffee and a breakfast platter that included pancakes, eggs, bacon, and sausage.

"What about you, honey?" the waitress asked me.

I had no clue what possessed me to do it, but I looked at Cruz.

And something happened in that moment.

The same thing that had happened in that alcove.

His eyes held mine for the longest time and I knew this time it would have to be my choice. My mind was telling me not to go there, but deep down in my belly, something began to loosen and unfurl the longer Cruz held my gaze.

It's okay to let go sometimes, Elliot. To let someone else shoulder the burden. Whether it's for a few minutes, a few hours, or even a lifetime – it doesn't make you weak. It doesn't mean you failed.

What I did next wasn't about the food. In truth, I didn't care what I ate. No, it was about something else. It was about giving myself permission to feel something I never had. To give to someone else the things that sometimes became too much for me to hang onto.

Giving it to Cruz was safe because I'd never see him again after tonight. I knew that in my heart. I wasn't sure what act of fate had decided to bring us together for the evening, but real life would return soon enough. I'd go back to getting everything right tomorrow. Tonight, I'd let Cruz do what he'd offered.

Take some of that burden.

And maybe I'd finally be able to breathe again.

I ignored the way the waitress was tapping her pen on her pad and kept my eyes latched on Cruz's. When I tilted my head just the slightest bit, he immediately said, "He'll have the same, but instead of sausage, give him another order of bacon."

I smiled at that and leaned back against the booth. As soon as the waitress left, I said, "I love bacon."

"I know," Cruz responded, his eyes twinkling.

"How?"

He leaned against the table, arms folded, like he was about to tell me a secret. I did the same.

"You have a tell when something excites you, did you know that?"

I shook my head, but before I could say anything, Cruz reached across the table and ran his fingers over one of my hands. I pulled in a breath, then swallowed hard.

"There it is," he said softly, his eyes on me.

"What? I swallow?" I asked stupidly.

The rough pads of Cruz's fingers felt so good against my skin that I barely managed to suppress a moan.

"That too," Cruz said with a chuckle. "But no, it's your eyes. They light up – like you're seeing something for the first time."

"So, I'm like Pavlov's dog?" I asked with a chuckle. "But instead of responding to the sound of a metronome, I hear the word bacon and I get all hopped up with excitement?"

"A metronome? I thought it was a bell."

I shook my head. "Classic mistake. He used a metronome." I flushed and said, "Sorry, I'm full of useless facts like that. In case you missed it, I'm a bit of a nerd."

Cruz began playing with one of my hands. His finger stroked up and down the length of each one of mine over and over.

"I'm finding I've got a serious thing for nerds... well, one nerd in particular," he said huskily.

I had no clue how long we sat there like that for before the waitress returned with our coffee. The interruption forced us apart and I leaned back in my seat until she left, then began preparing my coffee.

"So besides being able to kick my ass at trivia and your excellent costume selection choices, tell me what makes you tick."

I smiled. "Not even going to ease me in, huh?" I asked.

"If you haven't noticed, I'm not real good on easing anything," he said with a self-deprecating smile.

Thank God for that.

"Well, um, I guess you already know about the foundation, since you were at the benefit. What were you doing there, by the way? I don't recognize your name."

"Afraid I crashed it?" Cruz asked.

I chuckled. "No, it's just, in my line of work I tend to know who's who." I paused and let my eyes rake over him, finally feeling a little more confident as I took in his dark beauty. "Believe me, I would have remembered someone like you."

"I got my ticket from my employer. He and his wife couldn't attend, so they offered the tickets up to the first takers at work."

"What kind of work do you do?"

"Construction."

I nodded, but didn't comment.

"What?" he asked.

"Nothing."

"Nuh-uh, Elliot. Doesn't work like that. Not tonight, anyway."

I sighed. "You don't look like you work in construction. If I had to guess, I would have said you were a soldier... or a cop."

"What makes you say that?"

I forced my eyes up from where I'd been toying with my coffee cup. "You act relaxed, but I can tell you're aware of everything that's happening around us. When we came in, you picked this booth, even though there were some closer to the door. It's near the back exit, right? And you took that side so you could see anyone coming through the front door."

Cruz studied me for a long moment, his already dark eyes going even darker. "I was a soldier," he finally said.

Since I could tell Cruz wasn't much older than my own twenty-five years, I couldn't help but wonder why someone in his prime wasn't still in that line of work. But it wasn't any of my business.

"I received a medical discharge and never went back."

It shouldn't have surprised me that he knew what I'd been thinking. "Sorry," I said. "It's none of my business."

"Yes, it is," he said. "Trust goes two ways, Elliot. I can't expect you to hand over pieces of yourself and not give back the things that make me who I am."

My heart swelled at that, but I tried to quell the emotion. There was no way he was feeling what I was. Not yet.

Probably not ever.

I forced the self-doubt away and said, "What happened?"

Despite Cruz being someone who was always aware of his surroundings, he hadn't yet looked tense. Now, though, it was hard to miss. His shoulders straightened and I saw him raise his hand to his head before slowly pulling it back. The move was odd – like he was trying to break himself of a habit. He leaned forward in the booth again and said, "I was in Germany. We'd just finished a mission and were preparing to head home after our debriefing. I was in Special Forces."

I didn't pressure him to continue when he fell silent. But I did reach across the table to cover his hand with mine. His skin was cold, so I automatically gathered his hand up into mine and began rubbing. His other hand was buried in his lap, so I couldn't give it the same treatment.

"I was with some of the members of my unit at this bar, but I was tired so I decided to call it a night. I was heading back to my hotel when I was jumped in the alley behind this abandoned building nearby. There were too many of them to fight. I was in and out of consciousness from the beating, but they made sure I was awake when they shot me the first time... and the second."

If I hadn't been holding his hand between mine, I would have covered my mouth as the horror trickled through me.

"I was unconscious for the third shot. The kill shot. But the fuckers were drunk, so they missed," Cruz said as he pulled my hand up and pressed one of my fingers against his head. I could feel the scar that was just above his temple and hidden by his hair.

"Who?" I whispered in horror. "Why?"

"My own men."

"What?" I gasped in disbelief. "Why? Why would they do this?" I asked as I caressed the scar. In my mind, I knew he wasn't in any danger anymore, but in my heart, it was like it had just happened.

"It was to get back at someone else. Someone I loved and someone who loved me."

"Who?"

"My brother, Matias."

"You have a brother?"

Cruz nodded. "He's ten years older than me. He was the team leader. I didn't know it at the time, but he'd discovered that several of the guys on the team had sexually assaulted several village women and girls while on our mission. He'd already started the process of having them court-martialed. They were to be arrested as soon as we got back to the States. Somehow, they found out and came after me. They knew Matias would come looking for me, so they laid in wait for him, then jumped him. But their drunk asses weren't any match for him. He killed three of them, put three more in the hospital and the rest got away, only to be picked up later by the MPs."

I must have looked confused because he clarified, "Military Police."

"What happened to the survivors?"

"Prison for most of them. One of them, the ringleader, managed to get away. Probably had help."

"And you recovered," I said.

"Fit as a fiddle," he said with a smile, though for the first time since I'd met him, it didn't reach his eyes. He might have recovered physically, but I doubted he'd gotten past the betrayal, because I could see the darkness that lingered in his gaze.

"They betrayed you," I whispered.

"Yes," he said simply.

My nerves felt scraped raw by his story. The simple solution would have been to just remain silent, but I couldn't. It was like what he'd said earlier – what he'd given me was a gift.

One that I wasn't about to squander.

So, before I knew it, I was giving him another piece of myself when I admitted something only a few people in my life knew. "It happened to my father too, but he didn't walk away from it."

CHAPTER 4

Cruz

I hadn't told Elliot my story to get him to tell me his, but I liked knowing he trusted me enough to share the truth with me. Yes, I already knew the details, but I had no idea how it had affected him. And while it wasn't a necessary part of the job I was tasked with, I was done kidding myself.

He wasn't a job.

I'd known that even before I'd deliberately bumped into him at the benefit. But I hadn't had the balls to admit it. Of course, admitting it now solved nothing.

"Will you tell me about it?" I asked when Elliot seemed reluctant to continue.

"I never met him," Elliot said softly. "But I still miss him. That's crazy, isn't it?"

Elliot was still holding onto my hand with both of his, so I pulled one up to my lips and brushed a kiss over his knuckles. "Not even a little bit."

"He was a cop with Seattle PD. He and my dad had been together for a few years when they decided to have me."

"Your dad is the one who started the investment firm you work at?" I asked. "The one you mentioned in your speech tonight?"

Elliot nodded. "Sam. I call him Dad and I call my father Pop. His name was Mac."

I nodded, urging him to continue.

"Pop and Dad were overjoyed when they found a surrogate. I guess they'd planned to have two kids together. One would be Pop's biological kid and the other would be Dad's. Anyway, same-sex marriage wasn't legal back then, but they'd been together a long time... Pop was older and he told Dad that someday there'd be a time when the world caught up and the second it did, he'd get down on one knee and pop the question. But until that day came, my dad would pester Pop about where not to do it – like on the kiss-cam at a basketball game or something. It was a running joke between them," Elliot quickly added.

"I bet that's exactly the kind of place he would have done it," I said gently.

Elliot laughed. "That's what Dad would always say." He dropped his eyes momentarily before saying, "Those were the hardest times, you know? When he'd see or hear something that would remind him of Pop and he'd get caught between wanting to remember and wanting to forget."

It was my turn to toy with Elliot's hand in an attempt to soothe him.

"After Pop... after he died, my dad found it."

"Found what?"

"The ring," he whispered. "He was going through Pop's stuff trying to pick out a suit for him to be buried in and he found it in the pocket of the jacket Pop was planning to wear the following weekend when they celebrated their anniversary. It was inscribed with the words *No more waiting.*"

Elliot's voice thickened as he pulled one hand free of mine and wiped at his eyes. "He was tired of waiting for the world to catch up."

I nodded because, for once, I was having trouble coming up with the right words to say. My own throat was tight with emotion.

"My dad put the ring on and hasn't taken it off since." Elliot took a moment to gather his emotions and then said, "Pop was shot while responding to a home invasion. He had the suspects pinned down, but he was running out of ammo. His backup never showed, even though he called in several times saying he needed help. Even after he got hit with the first bullet, those," – Elliot's eyes filled with tears and his expression twisted into one of helpless rage – "those fucking assholes wouldn't come!" He wiped angrily at his face. "Dad used to tell me how much Pop loved his job, despite all the homophobic pricks who wanted him off the force. He just wanted to protect people, to have their backs. Even when no one had his."

Elliot managed to calm down enough to say, "He didn't even have a partner because the asshole he'd been mentoring was too much of a fucking coward to stand up to the blue wall." Elliot shook his head angrily. "You want to know the worst part? That cop... my father's partner" – he sneered that last word – "is a fucking hypocrite! He's gay. Yeah. He's in a relationship with two guys and has two kids. And he's the captain of the same precinct that let my father die."

The venom directed at Declan Barretti didn't surprise me in the least, and part of me even felt some rage on Elliot's behalf. But I also knew how young and scared Declan must have been back then. I'd done enough research on the man to know that it had just been him watching out for his younger sister who'd been dealing with her first bout of leukemia at the time. I'd been about Declan's age when I'd finally found the courage to come out to my own parents, and it hadn't been a good experience. Luckily, I'd had Matias to lean on.

Declan hadn't had anyone, from what I could tell.

But I wasn't here to defend Declan, and I knew the cop wasn't expecting me to take up his cause. He'd already accepted his failure when it had come to Mac, Sam, and Elliot. There likely wasn't any coming back from that.

Elliot had managed to settle down. "Thank you for telling me that," I said as I continued to soothe him with my touch. It seemed to work because he eventually smiled and instead of releasing my hands again to dash at his damp eyes, he bent his head and lifted his arms to wipe his face on his biceps.

"Sorry, I guess that wasn't exactly easing you into it either, huh?" he said with a chuckle.

I laughed and said, "Easing is overrated. Sometimes you just need to go in hard and fast." I gave him a lecherous wink, which caused him to bust out into a huge laugh that I felt all over my body. I loved that he didn't even care that everyone was looking at us as we both laughed so hard we were nearly in tears. When we both finally settled, I said, "So why the investment firm? Is it the nerd thing?" I asked.

Elliot relaxed and tugged his hands free when the waitress appeared with our food. He waited until she was gone before snagging a piece of bacon from his plate and taking a hefty bite. If watching him laugh was freeing, watching the pleasure that sifted across his features as he ate was practically orgasm-inducing. God, what would he look like in the throes of passion? He wouldn't be able to hide anything from me.

"No, I mean, I like numbers and stuff, but it just kind of made sense, I guess. My dad's partner in the business was planning on retiring and I knew my dad wanted me to take his place, so it just kind of happened."

"And the foundation?"

"I guess it was a way of remembering my father. Of not losing myself in the unfairness of it all. All he ever wanted to do was help people. Even the night he died, he was still protecting the couple who lived in that house. When he ran out of bullets, he went after the guys with his fists long enough that the couple could make a run for it."

"A hero to the end," I said. "Not a bad guy to want to emulate."

"No, not at all," Elliot agreed.

"So, do you love it?" I asked. "The investment banking stuff? Like you do the foundation?"

Elliot didn't seem surprised by my observation.

"Truth?" he asked.

I didn't bother telling him I always wanted him to tell me the truth, since that would have made me the biggest hypocrite in the world, so I merely nodded.

"I don't really know what my dad was like before he lost my father, but growing up, he just seemed like this machine to me, at least when it came to work. Don't get me wrong, he always made time for me, but he also worked himself to the bone. When I was a baby, he actually took me to work with him. There are pictures of him on conference calls while he's holding me in his arms and feeding me my bottle. The firm, it had always been successful, but after my father died, it just kind of exploded. I think my dad needed that."

"What, the success?"

Elliot shook his head. "Not exactly. It was like he needed to keep moving and even though the success meant more and more money, I think it was the endless work that kept him going. As I got older and became more independent, he just lost more and more of himself in his work. I felt like..."

When he didn't continue, I said, "You felt like you were losing him."

"Yes," Elliot said, his voice softening. "So, I started asking questions about his business. It was a safe topic for us, you know? He didn't talk about my father much and it was hard for him to sit still long enough to talk about what I was up to. But as soon as I asked about his work, the floodgates opened. Within a matter of weeks, I was interning at the firm after school and over the summer. And even though I didn't love it, I didn't care because I got him back."

I nodded in understanding. "That was all that mattered to you."

"Yeah," he said with a sigh as he picked at his food. "He took an early retirement about six months ago, so most of the responsibility is on me now. He's trusting me not to let it fail, you know?"

I didn't respond to that, but I did know. Because that simple statement answered a lot of questions for me. Elliot's connection to his dad had gotten wrapped up in the business and I doubted either man even saw it. If Elliot's fear of failing his father was as great as I suspected it was, it explained why letting go of even a fraction of the iron grip he had on his need for control was so hard for him – and why he needed it so very badly. Twenty-five straight years of being afraid to fail the one constant in your life was bad enough, but Elliot was just as worried about failing the father he'd never had the chance to know.

Since the topic of his parents was bringing him down, I changed the subject to safe ones and began peppering him with the more basic questions two people typically went through when they were on a first date. I easily answered every question he lobbed back at me and only hedged on the ones relating to my work. But even the lie by omission was enough to sour the food in my stomach. When it came time to pay the bill, it took only a single, firm, no-nonsense command for Elliot to put his wallet away. I paid the bill and then took his hand in mine before leading him from the diner. As we headed for the waterfront, the conversation became easy and light and I liked how Elliot became freer with his words and his body. He leaned into me as he spoke, he flirted here and there, and even when he fell into a thoughtful silence, he stayed with me by stroking his thumb over mine or giving my hand an extra squeeze.

It wasn't until we ended up in a busy ice cream shop that things changed.

Momentarily.

Since that was all I would allow.

It happened as soon as we entered. I'd dropped his hand long enough to open the door for him, but when I reached for it again with the intent of leading him to the end of the long line, he carefully eased his hand away. At my questioning look, he said, "It's okay, you don't have to."

If I hadn't seen the pain in his eyes, I'd have thought he was the one who had an issue with the public display of affection in the overly crowded shop. But clearly, he thought I was the one who'd have a problem with it.

I disabused him of that notion when I snagged his hand and then gently maneuvered his arm behind his back, forcing his body to press against mine to compensate for the move. Elliot's eyes lit up with a mix of surprise and desire and if we'd been anywhere else, I would have taken things a step further to make sure he was getting my message loud and clear. "We good?" I asked as I pressed my hips against his, not caring if we were putting on a show for the rest of the patrons.

Elliot managed a nod, but nothing more.

"Good," I said before leading him to the back of the line. I put him in front of me and wrapped my arms around his chest. I let my mouth nuzzle the side of his neck, then his ear. "We're going to talk about what just happened later."

Another nod.

We didn't speak again until we got up to the counter. Elliot eyed the dozens of flavors and asked to try several, but when he looked to me expectantly, I shook my head and laughed. I dropped my mouth to his ear and whispered, "You're going to have to help me out on this one because your eyes have lit up more times than a fucking Christmas tree since we got up here."

He grinned and then whispered his flavor choice in my ear. Then he discreetly pressed a kiss against it before drawing back. I managed to order for him and myself, and he didn't argue with me when I paid for the ice cream and collected our cones. We walked along the length of the pier as we ate our ice cream.

By the time we'd reached the end of it, we'd finished the treats. Before I could ask Elliot my next question, he said, "You've got a little ice cream right here," and then his finger came up to touch a spot on the corner of my mouth. Before I could reach up to take care of it, Elliot leaned forward and pressed the gentlest of kisses to the spot. "Thank you, Cruz," he said right before he pulled back. "I really needed this tonight."

I was too overwhelmed to speak. How had this man managed to tie me in knots so quickly?

Elliot turned and leaned against the end of the pier and I did the same. We didn't speak as we watched a ferry cross the bay and dock. We didn't talk, but we were still communicating in so many ways. Little touches, the occasional look, a soft smile.

It was during one of those emotion-filled looks Elliot sent my way

41

that I held his gaze with mine and when I turned toward him, he did the same. I saw the moment he knew what I was going to do, because his eyes did that thing. But even then, I didn't rush it. No, I just watched him for several beats, then used my fingers to tuck an errant lock of hair behind his ear. He was trembling, but he didn't move otherwise.

Not to pull away.

Not to lean toward me.

He was letting me lead… giving me the trust that I craved. When I finally dipped my head and my lips were nearly brushing his, he whispered in a rush, "I'm not good at this part."

His insecurity didn't surprise me in the least, so I paused only long enough to say, "Yes, you are," and then covered his mouth with mine. I swallowed his gasp of surprise and let my tongue slide into the deepest recesses of his mouth. He was stiff and unresponsive for all of two seconds, then he was kissing me back with all the passion I'd suspected was lying untapped inside of him. His arms curled around my neck at the same time I wrapped mine around his waist. I pulled him flush against me and, not caring who was watching, devoured his mouth as my hands roamed up and down his body.

Elliot was anything but passive during my sensual assault. No, he was returning every kiss with fervor and when I was forced to come up for air, his lips latched onto my neck. It was only when I heard a discreet cough that I remembered where we were and broke the kiss and forced some space between our bodies. I'd somehow managed to break my promise to myself to wait to taste him until we were some place where we wouldn't be interrupted.

But holy fuck, had it been worth it.

Elliot was completely oblivious to our surroundings as he fought to catch his breath. His hands were pressed against my chest and I had no doubt he could feel the desperate pounding of my heart. "You said you weren't going to do that tonight," he managed to get out.

"It's not tonight anymore, Elliot. It's after midnight, which means it's tomorrow."

Elliot chuckled and dropped his forehead to my shoulder. I put my hand against the back of his neck and pressed a kiss against his temple. "What were you saying about not being good at that part?" He didn't answer, just shook his head. But I wasn't willing to simply let it go, so I whispered into his ear, "If you get any better at that, you're going to send me to an early grave."

I could feel him smiling against me. When he pulled back, his eyes were bright with emotion. "Cruz," he said softly.

Just my name, but it was enough. It was the same as when he'd said my name for the first time back at the hotel. I could hear the unspoken question just as surely as if he'd yelled it into my ear.

"Are you sure, Elliot?" I asked. As badly as Elliot needed me to take control, there were some things I just needed to hear him say. Once we'd been together longer, I knew that wouldn't be the case...

The thought dropped off as cold reality intruded. There would be no together after he found out who I really was.

And he would find out.

Because I was going to tell him myself.

"Never been surer of anything. But... but I need it to be like it was at the hotel."

And there it was, in no uncertain terms.

"Where do you live?"

Elliot gave me the address and I realized it was within walking distance. But I was far too impatient. If I only had a few hours left with this man before I had to tell him who I really was, then I was going to take full advantage of it. "Your keys," I said as I held out my hand. Elliot dug his keys out of his pocket and handed them over without question. "Which one is for your apartment?" I asked.

"This one." He pointed to it and I nodded before sticking the keys in my pocket. Since it was too far to walk back to the hotel to get our cars, I said, "We'll take a cab."

"Can we stop by the bathroom? I need to wash my hands."

I nodded, though I suspected what he really needed was a moment to himself. Part of me didn't want to give it to him in case he changed his mind, but the other part knew that this choice was something he couldn't be regretting at any point. I led him down the pier and waited near the railing while he went into the public bathroom. It was a single bathroom, so I didn't have to worry about him encountering anyone in there.

I wasn't as lucky, because as soon as Elliot disappeared inside, a familiar voice said, "What are you doing, Cruz?"

I didn't bother looking at the man I knew was behind me.

"You were watching, Matias," I said to my brother. "You know what I was doing."

My brother leaned against the railing next to me. "This is dangerous," he said. "There are other ways to get close enough to him to keep him safe."

"You think I don't know that?" I murmured. It stung to know that my brother disapproved of what I was doing, but I couldn't explain the pull Elliot had on me, so how was I supposed to explain it to the man I'd idolized my entire life? The man who'd protected me from my father's fists? The big brother who'd shown up in that darkened alley just like my assailants had known he would?

"Then why?"

I looked at Matias. "Does it matter?"

"No, I suppose not," he responded.

I let my eyes rake over the brother who I no longer recognized. Physically, he hadn't changed much since we'd left the military. If anything, he was a little more heavily built than he had been, probably from all the extra hours he spent in the gym trying to burn off the rage and guilt he was feeling about the events of that night in the alley more than two years ago. But little else about him was familiar.

At ten years older than me, he'd never been an overly demonstrative kind of guy, but the coldness was new and something I'd never get used to. He never smiled anymore, never interacted with me beyond talking about the information relating to the cases we worked for Ronan together. We'd never talked about the night of the attack, and even after two years, he spent every free moment trying to find the single assailant who'd gotten away. The Matias I'd known growing up would have wanted to know what I was feeling – what Elliot was making me feel – but this Matias wouldn't care.

Because this Matias couldn't feel.

I decided to change the subject and said, "Anything?"

Matias had been following us from the moment we'd left the hotel. I'd planned it that way in order to give Elliot more of my attention so I could build a rapport with him. But the plan had never been to get *this* close.

"No," Matias said, then he was straightening. "Be careful, little brother," he murmured before he disappeared into the shadows again. Seconds later, Elliot came out of the bathroom. He was visibly nervous as he approached me.

"Ready?" I asked, fully prepared for him to tell me he'd changed his mind about what was about to happen.

"Ready," he said softly, then lifted his head just a little. I happily gave him what he wanted and settled my mouth on his. I kept the kiss relatively tame compared to the one we'd shared at the end of the pier and then took his hand in mine. Matias's words rang in my ear, but it didn't matter. I couldn't be careful because I was already in too deep.

But I couldn't bring myself to regret it.

CHAPTER 5

Elliot

*H*e was all over me in the cab and I couldn't have been happier about it. I'd tried protesting at first when Cruz had begun kissing me in the back seat and rubbing his hand up and down my thigh, but when he'd wrapped his fingers around my neck in a gentle grip and ordered me to keep my eyes on him, I'd forgotten all about the cab driver.

I hadn't been able to keep my eyes on him, but only because I couldn't keep them open. The things he was doing to me just felt so damn good.

I'd been kissed by a few guys over the years, but nothing they'd done compared to what Cruz was doing to me. It felt like my entire body was on fire.

But the best part?

I didn't have to fucking think.

About anything.

My mind was solely focused on Cruz and pleasing him by giving him what he wanted. Another guy might have taken advantage of that, but Cruz just turned it around and gave it all right back. Everything he did, everything he said, was about me.

About pleasing me.

About taking care of me.

He whispered things in my ear that no one had ever said to me before.

Like how beautiful I was.

Like how he couldn't wait to watch me come apart in his arms.

Like how lucky he was that he'd found me tonight.

"Cruz, please," I whispered against his mouth when his hand once again bypassed my dick. He'd been running his hand all over me, but ignoring the part that needed his touch the most.

"Soon, baby," he murmured, then kissed me gently. His hand stopped roving and I wanted to protest the loss, but I didn't want to risk losing the touch of his lips too. When he stopped kissing me a moment later, I tried to follow him. "We're here, Elliot," he said softly before taking my hand and leading me from the cab. I barely managed to greet my doorman as we made our way into the building, and judging from the surprised look the man gave me, I figured I probably looked like I'd actually gotten fucked in the back of that cab.

But I couldn't find it in me to care.

Once we were in the elevator, Cruz was on me again. His desperation to consume me drove my need higher and higher and I was pretty much a puddle of goo by the time we reached my floor. If Cruz hadn't been leading the way, I doubt I would have even been able to find my own damn apartment. The second Cruz got us inside my place, he slammed the door shut, tossed my keys to the floor and then pressed me up against the door.

White-hot heat flared through me when his fingers wrapped around my wrists and he pinned my arms to the door. He ground his cock against mine and grated out, "Feel that? That's all for you. You're going to fit me so good, Elliot. Like you were made just for me."

I managed a nod.

"Say it," he ordered harshly.

His tone had my need spiking to astronomical proportions. I was never going to last at this rate.

"Just for you," I said in a rush.

"Who do you belong to tonight, El?"

The nickname had me groaning out loud. "You, Cruz. Only you."

"You want my cock in that tight ass of yours, my boy?"

I nodded vigorously, since I wasn't sure I was even capable of speaking.

"Say it," Cruz demanded. His hold on my wrists was unforgiving and I loved every second of it.

"Yes!" I nearly shouted. "God, yes, I want it," I admitted. Emotion bombarded me as the need to give in completely warred with the voice in my head telling me I shouldn't be craving the rough treatment.

"Baby, open your eyes."

I did as he said. When had I even closed them?

"Look at me."

I shook my head. "Can't," I ground out.

"Look at me, Elliot."

There was no room in his voice for argument, so I did. His hold hadn't eased on me even a little bit, which I was grateful for.

"It's not wrong," Cruz said. "What's happening here... it's not wrong. It could never be wrong."

I managed a nod that I wasn't feeling, but not surprisingly, he called me on it. "It doesn't make you weak or disgusting or a freak."

I flinched at that and turned my eyes away from him. But he grabbed my chin and forced me to look at him again. "Who?" he asked. "Who told you it was wrong?"

"No... no one."

"Who?" he asked again.

I knew then that I was fighting a losing battle. And despite the fact that my lust had cooled somewhat, it was still there, simmering right below the surface.

"My first boyfriend."

"What did he say?"

"Cruz—"

"What did he say, Elliot?"

I was a goner when his hand slipped down to my throat. Shame crawled through me. "I... I always had trouble getting off with him. One day as he was... as we were..."

"Fucking," Cruz supplied.

"Yeah," I said, feeling foolish for not even being able to say the word. "He was behind me and I asked him... I asked him to hold me down by the back of the neck. He put his hand on my neck, but it wasn't hard enough. I could still..."

I shook my head because I just couldn't say the words out loud.

"Move," Cruz said.

I nodded.

"You couldn't let go," he added.

I could feel the tears stinging the backs of my eyes. "When I asked him to hold me harder, he got mad. He said I was a freak for being into that kind of shit. But I didn't... I wasn't..."

Cruz sighed and said, "Did you explain to him that you weren't asking him to cut off your air?"

I nodded. "I tried to tell him that it wasn't like that, but he wouldn't listen. Said I need to find some other sick fuck to do that shit to me. I think he thought... that I wanted... God, fuck," I whispered harshly. I tried to pull free of Cruz's hold as the humiliation washed over me, but he refused to let me go.

"He thought you wanted to play out a rape fantasy," Cruz murmured.

"I didn't!" I practically shouted. "I know some people like that, but that isn't it—"

Cruz kissed me long and hard. "I know that, and I know you aren't looking for breath play, either. You want to just be able to feel. You want someone to take away that noise in your head for a while."

"He was right," I whispered.

"He was a fool," Cruz shot back, his voice tipped with anger. "What you want isn't wrong, Elliot. Just like it isn't wrong that I think it's fucking beautiful. Let me prove it to you." He kissed me again, gently, almost reverently. I kissed him back and hoped it was answer enough.

He released my throat only long enough to pin my arms over my head with one hand before he returned his other hand to my neck. He kissed me hard as he applied just the right amount of pressure to my windpipe. The fear of failure instantly drained from my body and I drew on the strength of his fingers that were pressing into my skin. I had no idea how long he kissed me for, but my lust came rushing back to the surface within seconds. When I began squirming against him to try to brush our cocks together, he growled one simple order that had my dick leaking in my pants.

"Don't." When I instantly stopped moving, he continued, "Elliot, if at any time you want me to stop, you simply say the word stop. Do you understand?"

I nodded because I knew what he was doing, why he was bringing it up. It was a safe word. The very fact that he felt the need to have one both excited and humiliated me.

"It's only because I'm still learning what you need," Cruz explained. "I know that isn't the kind of relationship you're looking for."

The realization that he knew what I was thinking was both comforting and embarrassing. I'd never been drawn to the sexual lifestyle that included using pain to bring pleasure, and I had absolutely no desire to call Cruz sir or master or any other title that put a label on what we were doing.

"I don't want that kind of a relationship, either," he murmured against my mouth. "But I want you to know that giving up control doesn't mean you have none."

"Okay," I said. "I trust you, Cruz."

He smiled. "I know you do, baby. I'm gonna take good care of you and you're going to do the same for me, okay?"

I nodded, then kissed him. I was beyond talking. I was done obsessing over all of this. I was ready to do what Cruz was giving me permission to do.

Just feel.

CHAPTER 6

Cruz

It took just minutes to get Elliot back into the headspace he was craving. I wanted to kick the ass of the guy who'd made Elliot believe that him wanting rough sex and a little bit of dominance/submission play was the same as a full-on BDSM encounter. While there was nothing wrong with the latter for those who enjoyed that kind of sexual play, it was nothing like what Elliot wanted. At best, he was looking for someone he could give his choices away to long enough that his brain could focus on the pleasure. But instead of trying to figure out how to take the gift Elliot had given him, the fucker had twisted it into something ugly that had undoubtedly stayed with Elliot through every sexual encounter and relationship that had followed.

Elliot and I were both breathless when I released his mouth, then his hands. I kept my one hand on his throat as I held his gaze.

"When I release you, I want you to take off your clothes, then mine. I'm going to touch you while you do it, but you don't get to touch me any more than is absolutely necessary. Do you understand me?"

He swallowed hard and nodded. His pulse was thrumming beneath my hand. My dick hurt like a motherfucker, it was so desperate for relief.

I dropped my hand and Elliot immediately began to work his costume loose. I could see that his hands were shaking, but I suspected it wasn't just because of nerves. I didn't help him remove the costume, but as soon as the layers of fabric began hitting the floor, I did what I said I would and began touching him.

His body was even better than I'd imagined. He had a runner's body. Long and lean but well-muscled. His skin was pale compared to mine and I loved seeing the contrast of it. When Elliot was left with just his underwear, he hesitated for a moment and I knew that asshole ex's voice was in his head again.

"Eyes on me," I said firmly when Elliot refused to look at me as his fingers hovered on the waistband. He immediately lifted his gaze and then drew in a deep breath. Then the underwear was gone and he stood there nervously, his eyes never leaving mine.

"Keep them on me," I said. "I want you to see what I see when I look at you."

I let my eyes rake over his body, then followed with my hand. Elliot did exactly as I asked and kept his eyes on me the whole time.

Until I touched his cock. Then his eyes slid shut and he let out a ragged moan. He was leaking like a sieve from his dick.

"Open them," I demanded.

Elliot's eyes flipped open.

"Look at the proof of how badly your body wants this," I said. Elliot dropped his gaze and watched me collect some of his pre-cum on my finger. I made sure he was watching when I lifted my finger to my mouth and sucked it deep inside. He whimpered just as his lips parted. I pulled my finger slowly back out, collected more fluid, then lifted it to his lips. When he went to suck my finger into his mouth, I said, "No," and he promptly stopped. I spread the fluid on his lips, then sealed my mouth over his. I kissed him long and deep, then licked his lips before kissing him again.

A strangled moan tore from his lips. His arms went around my neck and he leaned into me as he hungrily kissed me back. I grabbed his ass with both my hands and pulled him forward so his cock was brushing mine. It took every ounce of self-discipline I had to break the kiss and say, "Undress me."

Unlike with his own costume, Elliot's fingers moved much more quickly this time around and he managed to follow my order of not touching me, though from the way his eyes scanned my body, I knew it was a command he wasn't happy about having to follow. I leaned down and whispered into his ear, "You'll get your chance to play, baby."

A tremor sifted through his body and his eyes glazed over. Knowing that he'd already reached a point where he was able to let go of everything but the need to feel had me experiencing a sense of pride in him that I couldn't explain. To give in to his need so quickly after years of being made to believe his needs were wrong was a testament to his strength. But I knew he wouldn't believe me if I told him that. I'd have to show him instead.

"On your knees, El," I murmured.

He quickly dropped to his knees, but didn't go for my dick like he clearly wanted. I carded my fingers through his hair and said, "You want a taste, baby?"

Elliot nodded frantically.

"Say it."

"Yes, I want to taste."

Instead of giving him permission, I took my dick and pressed the crown against his mouth. Pre-cum streaked across his lips as I toyed with him. When I pulled back, I said, "Lick your lips."

He did and then he closed his eyes in pleasure. I waited until he opened them again, then said, "Open your mouth."

His response was instantaneous and when I pushed deep into his mouth, he didn't protest. "Play with me, but don't make me come."

I'd barely finished the statement before Elliot went to town on my dick. His mouth was heaven and I cursed the fact that I was too close to enjoy it for more than a couple of minutes. I withdrew my dick from his mouth and then hauled him to his feet. I kissed him hard, tasting myself on his tongue. "Do you have condoms and lube in your room?"

"Yes," he said, his breath coming in heavy pants.

"Good." I reached down to grab the backs of his thighs. When I lifted him, he automatically wrapped his legs and arms around me. Then his mouth was on mine. Luckily his bedroom was easy to find because he wouldn't stop kissing me long enough to maneuver down the hallway. We both ended up laughing a few times when I bumped into the walls or hit my elbow on a sharp corner, but the levity was a good thing. Elliot was so relaxed that it was like he was a different person than the one who'd stood before me and had admitted to being called out as a freak for having needs that might not have necessarily been considered the norm.

Once inside Elliot's room, I lowered him to his back on the bed and followed him down. I made out with him for several long minutes and then played with his body for a while. I used my mouth and hands to drive him wild, but I bypassed his dick until he was literally begging me.

"What do you want, baby?" I asked when he called my name for the third time.

"I wanna fuck your mouth."

I smiled at the demand. If Elliot could only see himself now. He'd made this assumption that this night would be about me controlling him and determining everything we did, but here he was, so lost in what he was feeling that he was making his own demands. I doubted he was even aware of it. I gave him what he wanted and sucked him to the back of my throat, but from the way his cock was pulsing, I knew he'd blow if I wasn't careful. I teased him with light sucks and licks and ignored both his pleas for more and the way he was trying to force my mouth down on his length.

I rose to my feet and said, "Condoms, lube."

"There," he said, his voice sounding ragged. He pointed to his nightstand drawer. As I worked a condom down my shaft, I admired Elliot's body as he lay splayed out for me on the bed like the most decadent of dishes. There was absolutely no shame in his expression as I watched him.

"Turn over," I said as I reached for the lube. He was so focused on my dick that it took him a moment to follow the order. "On all fours," I said as I stepped into position behind him. He did what I said.

"Spread your legs wider. Show me that pretty hole. Let's see how badly it wants my cock."

Elliot moaned, but complied. I was putting him in the most vulnerable of positions, but he did it without hesitation. His backside was gorgeous and my mouth watered at the sight of his fluttering entrance. I couldn't stop myself from leaning down and running the flat of my tongue over it. Elliot let out a hoarse shout and bucked away from me, but I was ready for the move and I grabbed his hips.

"Cruz, what are you—"

His words died off into a strangled groan when I licked him again. He fought me for another second or two, undoubtedly because he'd never had this done to him before, then he was pressing back on my mouth. His hand began frantically stroking his dick. I reached between his legs to knock his hand away and lifted my mouth from his hole long enough to say, "Whose cock is this?" I gave his dick a hard tug and he cried out.

"Whose?"

"Yours!"

Satisfied that he wouldn't touch himself again, I went to town on his ass. My plan had been to prep him with my fingers, but I knew we were both way too close for that. I had to hope his hole was loose enough from the attention I'd given it, because I was done waiting.

"Drop your shoulders to the bed, but keep your ass here," I said as I gently slapped Elliot's writhing ass. He groaned and did as I said. I got into position between his legs so that I was standing on the floor while he was kneeling on the bed. I placed my cock at his opening and began pushing and was pleased when Elliot bore down on me. I took my time working myself inside of him, determining my forward progress based on his body's responses. He was moaning and crying out, but none of the noises he made had anything to do with pain or fear. By the time I bottomed out, we were both sweating and shaking. My own control was frayed beyond belief, but I knew I needed to hang onto it a little longer. Elliot still needed that last little bit from me – that thing that would truly set him free and show him just how right all of this really was.

I began fucking him with slow, easy glides to let him adjust, but when his inner muscles began clamping down on me, I knew he was ready. I reached down to grab both his arms and pinned them behind his back. I used one of my hands to hold them in place, leaving him completely at my mercy. But it wasn't enough.

I leaned over his back and sought out his mouth. "Gonna give you what you need, baby. Gonna show you how beautiful you are like this, how perfect."

He kissed me back. I could see he was really close to that place in his mind where nothing else existed but the need to come.

"Yes," Elliot whispered, his voice heavy with unshed tears. It was proof of how emotional this experience was for him.

I settled my free hand on the back of his neck. The position meant Elliot was supporting a good amount of my weight as I thrust into him and he was truly helpless. Even if he'd wanted to, he couldn't have moved on his own. He was completely at my mercy.

I rocked into him gently a few times to let him get used to the position, then picked up the pace. His body was so tight around my dick that I was sure I'd blow before he did. I began hammering into him as I added more pressure to his neck. I also didn't let up on his hands at all and I could feel them flexing between our bodies.

"Is this what you want, my boy?" I asked as I began pounding Elliot hard and fast. The hold I had on him rendered him completely immobile. He couldn't even move his head.

"Yes!" he cried out. There was no mistaking the tears now because he was practically sobbing as I rutted into him. "Please, Cruz, harder!" he begged. His desperation drove me to new heights and my control snapped. I slammed into him harder than I probably should have, but his keening cries of pleasure just drove me on. Pure pleasure radiated through my body as the pressure in my balls began to build and build.

"So fucking close," I ground out. I knew I had just seconds left, so I released Elliot's hands and then slid my hand around to the front of his throat. I gripped him hard and pulled him to an upright position so that he was on his knees in front of me. His hands came up to grab the arm I was using to hold onto his throat, but he didn't try to free himself.

No, he was clinging to me.

"Jesus," I whispered. I reached my free hand around Elliot's front and closed it over his weeping dick. I began stroking him hard and fast to match my thrusts into his body.

He began screaming my name as he rode the edge of the orgasm, but it wasn't until I whispered, "Come for me, baby," in his ear and then gently bit down on the spot where his neck met his collarbone that he shouted in relief. I felt his release hit the arm I had wrapped around his upper body, then it was sliding down my hand. Elliot's sobs of relief tore at my insides and I came hard and fast. I released his dick so I could wrap my arm around his waist to hold him in place while I fucked into him with a final few hard thrusts. The orgasm was blinding in its intensity and there was a point where it felt like I was going to pass out. It had to be at least two full minutes before I came back to myself enough to loosen the hold I had on Elliot's neck. He sagged against my arm and I carefully lowered him to the bed, then followed him down until most of my weight was pressing him into the mattress. We were both still breathing hard, but I managed to press gentle kisses into his skin wherever I could reach without having to release him.

Time slowed after that. We somehow managed a shower together before falling into his bed. No words were spoken, but I knew neither of us needed them. Our bodies had said it all and then some. Elliot was asleep within minutes of me turning out the light on his night-stand. I had no clue how long I managed to keep my eyes open as I enjoyed the press of Elliot's body against mine, but when I next became aware of my surroundings, it was still dark outside and I was alone in bed. I glanced at the clock on the nightstand and saw that it was four in the morning. I went searching for Elliot and found him working on his computer in the living room. I didn't miss the tension in his shoulders. He was writing notes on a small notepad.

"Elliot?"

He startled briefly, then turned to look over his shoulder at me. "I'm sorry, did I wake you?"

I shook my head. "No, just missing you," I said truthfully.

He smiled at that and said, "Sorry, I just had to check something for work."

"Everything okay?" I asked as I took in his pinched features.

"Um, yeah... no..." He shook his head and laughed lightly. "Sorry. It's just, some money went missing from this client's account and it's just this big, fucked-up mess."

I stiffened at his words as I realized he very well could have just inadvertently given me the information I needed. Before I could question him further, he closed the laptop and set it and the notebook on the coffee table. "Let's go back to sleep," he said. "I can look at it with fresher eyes in a few hours."

I nodded and held out my hand to him. He took it and walked around the couch. There was no hesitation on his part when he kissed me. When he pulled back a little, it was just to study me for a moment before he wrapped his arms around me. He laid his head on my chest and I immediately put an arm around him and then let my free hand stroke his hair.

"It's real, right, Cruz? What we did last night. This. You feel it too, right?"

"I do, El," I whispered before leaning down to press a kiss to the top of his head. "It's real."

He nodded. "Good."

I led him back to bed, and even though he needed to sleep, I couldn't stop myself from making love to him again. This time it was slow and gentle and I took him from the front so that I could see the play of emotions in his eyes. Satisfaction went through me when it became clear that he didn't need me to control our pleasure this time around. I knew there would be days when it would be like this and there would be times where it would be like the first time. And I was looking forward to every single one. I just had to figure out how to make it happen.

After Elliot fell asleep, I eased myself out of bed and went to the living room. I searched out my phone and snapped a picture of the notes Elliot had taken about the client with the missing money. I sent the picture to both Memphis and Declan, then went back to bed. As I pulled Elliot into my arms, I debated when to tell him the truth.

Because I needed this job to be over.

So that what I really wanted to have with him could begin.

CHAPTER 7

Elliot

*J*t was the dreaded morning after. I'd been awake for almost an hour, but I hadn't been able to focus on much of anything as I waited for Cruz to wake up. I'd spent a little more time working on the White account, but what I'd found had only caused more questions than answers. Add in the fact that I had no clue what was going to happen when Cruz walked out of my bedroom, and I was a mess.

The sex the night before and early this morning had been nothing short of a miracle in my mind. I'd never experienced anything in my entire life like I'd felt when I'd come. The fact that I'd cried like a baby over something as simple as an orgasm should have sent Cruz running from the room, but no, he'd stayed. And then he'd made love to me again.

And he'd said it was real.

It *was* real.

I couldn't deny it anymore. I didn't want to.

Whatever Cruz had unlocked inside of me was never going to go back in its cage. If I was a freak like my college boyfriend had said I was, then so be it. I'd rather be a freak in Cruz's arms then a normal man outside of them.

I flinched when I heard my bedroom door open, but I stayed where I was, despite the need to flee. If he said his goodbyes and just left, I'd deal with it. It would suck, but I'd deal, and I'd at least have the memories of the night before to hold onto for a while... or forever.

But my fears were waylaid the second he stepped into the kitchen and sealed his mouth over mine. He tasted of mint and I wondered if he'd used my toothbrush to brush his teeth, since I didn't have a spare. I really wanted to believe that he had.

I didn't know why.

I couldn't help but smile against his mouth, which caused him to smile. "What?" he asked.

"Nothing."

"Definitely not nothing," he said.

"You'll think I'm crazy," I replied.

"And?"

That simple question was enough to settle the butterflies dancing around in my belly.

"I was wondering if you used my toothbrush... I'm kind of hoping you did."

Cruz smiled and swiped his thumb over my chin. "Hope no more," he murmured. Then his mouth was back on mine and the passion flared between us. He was the one to put some space between our desperate bodies. He shook his head at me. "You're a dangerous man, Elliot Wittier."

I smiled and motioned over my shoulder. "There's coffee."

"Thanks." Cruz sat down next to me at the kitchen table a minute later with a cup of coffee in hand. "Did you figure that stuff out with your client?"

"Sort of," I hedged.

"You want to talk about it?" he asked knowingly.

"I haven't found the money, but I know who moved it from the account. But it doesn't make sense."

"Why not?"

I hesitated before admitting something I was still struggling with. "It was my dad."

"Your dad?"

I nodded.

"I thought you said he retired."

"He did – he doesn't have a hand in the day-to-day operations and even while he was still at the company, he didn't do account operations. We have people for that. Every employee has a code that gets logged when a transaction is made. My dad's code is attached to the withdrawal of the money from the account."

"Did you ask him about it?" Cruz asked as he carefully sipped his coffee.

"I'm going to tonight. I'm heading over there later to take my brother trick-or-treating."

Cruz stopped mid-sip and said, "You have a brother?"

I chewed on my lip for a moment and said, "Yeah. Ryan. He's nine. My dad adopted him six months ago. He was doing some work for this charity in Europe and he stopped by an orphanage. He met Ryan and just knew that he was meant to be his son. Ryan, he's got cerebral palsy. If my dad hadn't found him, he probably never would have gotten out of that orphanage."

"Wow, that's amazing," Cruz said. "Is that why your dad retired early? To take care of Ryan?"

I nodded. "Ryan's confined to a wheelchair and he has limited speech – he uses this computer to communicate. He's such a great kid, Cruz. Even though he can't talk, he's got this personality on him like you wouldn't believe. It's been incredible to watch it come to the surface since my dad brought him home. And my dad... he's finally started to come alive again."

Cruz reached out his hand to cradle my cheek. He held me like that for a moment before saying, "Do you think I could meet them someday? Your dad and Ryan?"

I bit into my lip and nodded. "Actually, I was going to see if you wanted to come trick-or-treating with us. Dad's going to stay home and hand out candy. We could maybe do a late dinner or something afterward."

I hated that I was too afraid to admit what I was really feeling – that I wasn't ready for this to end yet. But Cruz didn't press me on it. Instead, he said, "I'd love to. How about we stop by my place so I can change and then maybe we can grab lunch?"

"Yes," I said without hesitation. "I'd love that."

"Good," Cruz said. He gave me a quick kiss and then rose. "You mind if I use your shower?"

I had no clue what possessed me to do it but I responded with, "Do you mind if I join you?"

"I was pretty much counting on it," Cruz said, his eyes twinkling with amusement.

"Then no, I don't mind," I said as I stood up. He took my hand and pressed a kiss into the palm before leading me toward my room.

And just like that, I lost another piece of my heart to Cruz de la Vega.

~

I watched in wonderment as Cruz knelt in front of Ryan's wheelchair and began talking to him like he'd been doing it for a lifetime. There'd been a little bit of nervousness on Cruz's part early in the evening when we'd arrived at my dad's house, but he'd adjusted quickly and within minutes of meeting Ryan, he'd picked up on how to interact with my brother. He'd spoken to him like a regular little boy, not a child with a disability, which Ryan had definitely responded to because he'd opened up to Cruz much more quickly than he normally did with strangers. My dad had been hovering by Ryan's side protectively at first, but as soon as he'd realized Ryan was okay with Cruz, he'd joined me in the kitchen where I'd been putting the final touches on Ryan's costume. I'd wanted to ask my dad about the missing money from the White account, but he'd accosted me with questions about Cruz instead. And when Cruz had shot me a warm look from where he'd been sitting in the living room talking to Ryan, I'd pretty much been a goner and my dad had seen it. I had no doubt that just as soon as he managed to get me alone, he'd be peppering me for more information.

Not that I had that much to give, although it was more than I'd had this morning.

During and after lunch, Cruz had told me about his family and childhood. Both he and his brother had been born in Colombia, but had immigrated to the US with their parents when Cruz was just a baby. The stories I'd heard lent themselves to the fact that Cruz's childhood hadn't been an easy one, and while he hadn't come right out and admitted it, I suspected he and his brother had been abused. Between his less-than-perfect childhood and the scars I'd seen this morning on his body as we'd showered – the remnants of the brutal attack he'd endured two years earlier – I was in awe of how grounded the man was. I wondered if a lot of that had to do with his brother, since Matias had been the topic of many of Cruz's stories. Cruz had admitted that his brother hadn't been the same after the attack, but we hadn't had the time to really talk about it much. It was a topic I definitely wanted to come back to, since it clearly was causing Cruz a lot of pain.

"I think we cleaned them out," Cruz said as he and Ryan reached me where I was standing on the curb. Since most of the houses in my dad's neighborhood had steps leading up to the front door, many of the homeowners had come down to meet us on the walkways leading from the sidewalk to the houses to give Ryan his candy after he used his computer to say, "Trick or Treat." For those few people that hadn't come to us, Cruz had done the most amazing thing. He'd gently picked my brother up out of his chair and then trotted up to the door with him and then chimed the phrase on my brother's behalf. I'd been able to tell just from my brother's garbled laugh that he'd loved it.

"Did you get a good haul?" I asked Ryan.

"Big time," came the response from his computer. I leaned down to drop a kiss to his head. I'd fallen as in love with my brother as my dad had, and I lived for these moments where he was just a regular little boy.

"Good," I said. "Let's go home and see how you made out."

Ryan held out his hand in what I knew was his high-five motion. I gently smacked my palm against his, then watched Cruz do the same. I reached for Cruz's hand as we began heading back to the house. I loved that he never hesitated to show me affection in public. There were lots of things about Cruz de la Vega I was coming to love and I knew it was just a matter of time before I lost my entire heart to him. I had to remind myself that such a thing wasn't possible, but then I remembered my dad's words to me when I'd once asked him what it was like to fall in love. I'd foolishly thought maybe I'd felt that way about my first boyfriend, before the whole freak thing.

You just know, Elliot. I knew with your father the very moment I laid eyes on him. Didn't matter how many people told me love at first sight was just a myth. I was as much in love with your father on the day he died as I was on the day we met.

"Thanks for tonight," I said.

"The night's not over," Cruz reminded me.

"No... no, it's not," I said with a smile.

It took just a few minutes to round the last corner before my dad's house. My focus was on Ryan as he maneuvered his wheelchair up the walkway, so I didn't notice the car and the man standing next to it at first. But when I did, I recognized him instantly and came to a grinding halt.

Declan Barretti.

"What are you doing here?" I asked as the familiar cold went through me. My father was dead because of this man. He might not have pulled the trigger and he might not have been the one who'd ignored my father's pleas for help, but he'd condemned him to death just the same.

"I need to talk to you and your father."

I knew I was probably squeezing Cruz's hand too hard, so I turned to send him a silent apology, but found that he wasn't looking at me at all. His eyes were on Declan and his mouth was pulled into a tight frown.

Worried that he'd figured out who Declan was and that he might go after the man, I started to step between them, but stopped suddenly when Declan said, "I'm sorry, Cruz. It couldn't wait."

A chill ran down my spine when he said Cruz's name. The way he'd spoken to him, it was like… he knew him.

"You two… you two know each other?" I asked, though I wasn't sure which man I was even asking.

"Let's go inside, Elliot. It's safer to talk in there," Cruz said calmly.

I dropped his hand as if I'd been burned. Why the hell wasn't he denying it?

"No," I whispered, as understanding slowly dawned. "No," I said again with a shake of my head.

Cruz grabbed my upper arms in a firm hold. "Elliot, look at me—"

"No!" I spat out as I tore free from him. "How do you know each other?"

Cruz was clearly agitated and looked from Declan to me and back to Declan again. When Declan nodded, Cruz said, "Declan asked me to keep an eye on you after you were attacked a couple of nights ago. He was worried for your safety."

Bile crawled up my throat as I realized what he was saying.

"Oh my God," I whispered as I took a step back. Then another. "Oh my God," I repeated dumbly as things began to click into place.

"Elliot," Cruz said as he approached me, but the second he touched me, I lashed out at him. "Don't you touch me!" I screamed. I hit him in the chest, but all it did was hurt the hell out of my hand.

"Elliot?"

My dad's voice broke through the terrible keening sound that was piercing my brain. Then he was there, his strong arms going around me. "What did you do to him?" A moment later, he said, "You! What the hell are you doing here?"

I forced myself to pull free of my dad's arms. "Dad, let's go inside," I said. My only thought was getting my dad away from the man who'd destroyed our lives with one act of cowardice and the man who'd just destroyed my heart with his lies. I looked around for Ryan and saw that he was still up near the front door. He was clearly upset and confused by what was happening.

"Sam, Elliot, I'm afraid I need to talk to you," Declan said.

"Go to hell," my dad snapped. "You've done enough."

I took my father's arm and began walking up the walkway, but Declan's next words stopped me cold.

"Elliot, Edward White is dead. So are the two men who attacked you two nights ago."

"What?" I managed to get out. I could see that Cruz was just as surprised by the news as me.

"Elliot, what is he talking about? What men? The ones who vandalized the foundation?" My dad was completely confused, though I wasn't far behind him.

"Please, let's take this inside," Declan implored and I finally nodded. There were still a few people out and about, on their way home from trick-or-treating, no doubt. My father and I hurried up the walkway to calm Ryan down. Once inside the house, my dad got Ryan settled in his room with his favorite movie. I'd retreated to one corner of the living room in an attempt to get as far away from Cruz as I could. I felt like I was going to throw up.

He'd lied to me.

The whole thing had been a carefully orchestrated lie.

My body felt cold so I wrapped my arms around myself.

The things I'd said to him. The things I'd let him do to me. I automatically lifted my eyes to look at Cruz – to see if I could see how I'd missed the truth so easily – but I nearly stopped breathing when I found his eyes on me. And I could tell he knew what I was thinking.

"It wasn't, El," he said softly. "I swear it wasn't. Not all of it."

I laughed. It was an ugly, almost inhuman sound. Was he really expecting the fact that it supposedly hadn't all been a lie to make me feel better? "I don't believe you," I said simply.

"Talk," I heard my dad say as he reentered the room. On most days, my dad was a pretty easygoing guy, but I'd never seen him angrier. If looks could kill, Declan would be six feet under. Cruz probably would, too.

"After Elliot was attacked the other night, I was worried that there was something he wasn't telling me about the whole thing when my officers and I questioned him," Declan began.

My dad's gaze shifted to me. "Was there?" he asked.

I nodded. "I told him that I walked in on the guys, but they followed me in. They had a message for me," I said.

My father's anger slipped away and was replaced with concern. "What message?"

"They told me it was a mistake to steal from someone named White. They said I had three days to get him his money back."

"Why didn't you tell me?" Declan asked. "I could have helped you."

"Like you helped my father?" I asked.

The man instantly paled and I felt a surprising pang of guilt.

"Elliot," Cruz said. I forced myself to look at him, even though it hurt like hell. "I get it, okay?" he said. "Declan gets it too. He fucked up. But he couldn't have known what would happen to your father. He was a scared kid who probably has a story just like you do," he said. He glanced at my dad. "Like we all do."

I wanted to disagree with him, but deep down I knew there was logic to his argument. It didn't ease the hurt, but lashing out at Declan Barretti didn't, either. And it didn't bring my father back.

"I figured I could find out what happened to the money and return it and everything would be fine," I said to Declan. I looked at my dad and said, "I didn't find the money, but the transaction to move the money out of the account had your authorization code on it."

My dad shook his head. "That's impossible. I haven't even logged into the system in months."

"Did anyone have access to your code?" Cruz asked.

"No," my dad said, but then hesitated. "Blake… Blake did."

I knew who he was talking about almost instantly. Blake Dierenger had been my dad's assistant at one point. He'd become a junior Investment Associate after my dad had retired. But someone at that level had no reason to be accessing an account like the White one. And certainly not with my dad's credentials.

"Why would he—" My father's voice dropped off and he frowned.

I turned my attention to Declan. "You said you found Mr. White and his men dead?" I asked. "How did you even know to look for them?"

Declan's eyes dropped to the ground, which was answer enough. But Cruz confirmed it a moment later when he said, "I sent him a picture of your notepad from last night."

My knees felt weak and I had to sit down in a nearby armchair. God, I'd been such a complete fool.

"When I got the information from Cruz, I began investigating and discovered that Edward White was really a man named Edward Turnvall. He had an extensive arrest record including extortion, racketeering, assault, and money laundering. There was an outstanding warrant on him, so I took some officers to the address he used for his account with you. We found his body, along with those of two men fitting the descriptions you gave me, in the garage of his townhouse. It looked like they were ambushed as they were getting out of their car. They probably never saw it coming."

Declan's gaze shifted to my dad. "I'd like to put you and your family in protective custody until we figure out what happened. There's a possibility that the deaths had nothing to do with the missing money, but it's not worth taking a chance."

I saw my dad nod. "Yes, alright." I knew how hard it must have been for him to accept the offer, but he had bigger priorities than his hatred of Declan Barretti.

"Good, I'll—"

That was as far as Declan got before a computerized voice interrupted with a simple, "Daddy." Before my dad could go check on my brother, Ryan's wheelchair rounded the corner from the hallway leading to his room.

But my little brother wasn't alone.

No, standing right behind him with a gun pointed at the little boy's head was Blake Dierenger, my father's former assistant.

CHAPTER 8

Cruz

*T*he entire room went completely silent at the sight of the man holding the gun to Ryan's head. The boy was clearly confused and agitated. He kept pushing the lever on his wheelchair to make it go forward, but I suspected the man had switched it to manual so Ryan couldn't control the chair.

"Blake, what are you doing?" Sam croaked. He was standing next to me. I grabbed his arm as soon as he started heading for his son. Blake ignored Sam and pointed his gun at Declan, who'd been discreetly trying to go for his own weapon.

"No guns!" Blake shouted, his voice high and shaky. "Drop it!"

If I'd been armed, I could have taken him out then and there, but I hadn't wanted to risk Elliot discovering a weapon on me, so I wasn't carrying one. I hadn't really needed it, since I'd had Matias to back me up.

The thought of my brother had me desperate to reach my phone. I hadn't seen him out on the street when Declan had arrived, but that didn't mean he hadn't been watching. If I could activate my phone and speed dial him, he'd be able to hear the conversation that was happening. But my plan went up in smoke when Blake said, "Phones, too! Everyone drop their phones."

One by one, we tossed our phones toward the center of the room where Declan had dropped his gun. I suspected he had one at his ankle too, but it would be harder to get to, and since Blake was so shaky, chances were his own gun would go off if he was even remotely startled.

"Ryan, Daddy and the grown-ups need to talk. Can you be real quiet for a little while and then we'll go through your candy?"

Ryan's uncoordinated hand reached out to press the touchscreen of his computer. "Yes, Daddy."

"Blake, what are you doing here?" Sam asked as calmly as he could. He had his hands up.

The sound of Sam's voice talking to him did something strange to Blake. It actually seemed to relax him and he smiled at the older man. "Sam, I'm sorry it had to be like this, but I didn't have a choice. I... I wanted to give you more time, but things fell apart and I've done something and we have to go now."

Sam's eyes shifted briefly to Declan, then Elliot. "What are you talking about, Blake? Can you put the gun away? It's scaring Ryan and I know you don't want that."

The comment actually seemed to register for Blake because he nodded and dropped his hand to Ryan's shoulder. "I'd never hurt your boy, Sam. You know that."

His statement was in direct contrast to the fact that he still had the gun pointed at Ryan's head. I just couldn't tell if it was intentional or not. It didn't really matter, since one slip of his finger and the thing would go off.

"I packed his things, Sam. But we need to go."

Blake motioned to a backpack strapped to the back of the wheelchair. Between the way Blake's eyes were glazed over and his demeanor, I knew he wasn't right in the head. Which made him even more dangerous. I glanced at Declan and he nodded subtly. He'd noticed the same things I had.

"Go where?" Sam asked.

"Wherever you want, Sam," Blake said. "I've got lots of money now. You don't have to worry anymore. I can take care of you and Ryan, too."

I could hear the helplessness in Sam's voice as he said, "I don't understand, Blake."

Blake grew even more frustrated and waved his hand impatiently. Sam and Elliot gasped at the same time. "We can finally be together!" he declared.

"Dad," Elliot cut in before Sam could say anything else. "It's like you wanted," he said softly. "Blake feels the same way as you. Isn't that right, Blake?" he asked the younger man. "You love my dad, right? You took that money so you and he could finally be together, after all these years."

Blake nodded eagerly. He turned his adoring eyes to Sam. "I wanted to tell you so many times," he whispered.

Sam had finally caught on. "I know, but it was never the right time."

"No," Blake agreed. "I... I killed those men, but I don't know who else knows. So we have to go."

"Okay, but can you come to my room with me and help me pack? I'm not sure what I need to bring."

"No, I have to take care of them," he said as he waved his gun at the rest of us. His gun landed on Declan, but when his finger went for the trigger, Sam stepped between the two men.

"Dad," Elliot cried out, but Sam managed to ignore him.

"They're not going to tell anyone, Blake," the older man said patiently. "They want this for us."

Blake shook his head. "No, I'm in trouble."

"No, you're not," I cut in. "Everyone here knows why you did it. To protect Sam. To take care of Sam. You can't get in trouble for hurting someone to protect someone."

Blake looked at me in confusion as if he was really considering my words. He suddenly raised his hand that was holding the gun and hit his temple with it. "No!" he snapped. I saw the emotion leave his eyes the second his gaze settled on Elliot. "You did this! You told them about me!" And just like that, Blake dropped his arm and aimed at Elliot with a suddenly steady hand.

"No!" I screamed as I lunged for Blake, but I knew I was too far away to reach him. The gun went off and then, almost instantly, he fired again. But the recoil from the first shot caused his aim to go wide and I managed to throw all my weight against Sam, knocking him to the ground before the second bullet could hit him. Pain seared across my bicep, but I ignored it and staggered to my feet. Blake was already pulling the trigger again, the gun aimed square at Ryan, when a pair of hands appeared behind the man. Just as Sam screamed his son's name, my brother's hands wrapped around Blake's throat and in one swift move, he twisted Blake's neck until there was a sickening, cracking sound. Blake's body crumpled to the floor, the gun falling to the ground next to him. Sam scrambled to his feet and rushed to Ryan, who was making what I could only describe as screaming sounds. The boy's arms were flailing in front of his face as his father gathered him in his arms.

I frantically climbed to my feet and turned to check on Elliot. My heart nearly stopped at the sight of the two motionless bodies in the corner of the living room. "Elliot!" I screamed as I stumbled across the room. Declan's body was lying on top of Elliot's and there was blood pouring from a wound on his upper back.

I was just reaching for Declan when I saw Elliot move. "Help me get him up, Cruz," Elliot croaked as he tried to maneuver Declan's body.

The relief at hearing Elliot's voice was palpable, but I couldn't dwell on it. I eased my arms under Declan's shoulders and helped Elliot lift him. More blood poured from the wound. "Let's lay him on his side," I said. Elliot worked to free his legs from beneath Declan's body, then he was kneeling next to the fallen man. His eyes searched out his dad and brother and I heard him let out a rush of air when he saw they were unharmed.

Matias appeared at my side a moment later and helped hold Declan in place while I pressed my hand against the bullet wound. "Feel for a pulse," I told Matias. To Elliot I said, "Are you hurt?"

He shook his head. "No, he... just him. Fuck, Cruz, he took the bullet for me," he whispered. His hands were shaking as he said to my brother, "Do you have a phone?"

Matias quickly handed his phone over before saying to me, "He's got a pulse. There's a wound on his head – looks like he might have caught the edge of that end table as he was going down. Could explain why he's out."

Elliot's voice was panicked as he spoke into the phone. "Um, yes, we need help. There's been a shooting at my house. There's a police officer here. He got shot. His name is Declan Barretti." He choked back a sob and said, "Can you get someone here right away to help him? Please?" I wanted so badly to comfort Elliot and to assure him Declan would be all right, but I couldn't risk taking my hands off Declan's wound. The blood seemed to be slowing, and shortly after Elliot hung up the phone, Declan moaned.

"I'll call Ronan," Matias said as he took his phone back.

"Declan, can you hear me?" Elliot asked as he used his sleeve to wipe at some blood that was trickling down Declan's forehead from the cut along his temple.

"Elliot!" Sam called and then he was at our sides, Ryan in his arms. The boy was flailing in his father's hold, but he wasn't crying anymore, so I suspected it was just part of the disorder that caused his limbs to move uncontrollably.

"I'm okay, Dad," Elliot said as his father embraced him.

Sam was completely panic-stricken as his eyes raked over his oldest son, then his youngest. It was only then that he managed to take a breath.

"Cruz," I heard Declan say.

"Yeah, I'm here, Declan. Lie still, okay? You've been shot. Paramedics are on the way."

"Elliot?"

"I'm fine, Declan," Elliot said softly and put his hand on Declan's arm. "I'm right here. Dad and Ryan are okay too."

"Shooter?" he whispered, his voice full of pain.

"He's down," I said. "Situation's been neutralized."

Declan managed a nod. "My phone. I need to talk to my husbands. They'll worry."

Elliot scrambled up and got Declan's phone. He entered the code Declan told him and then found the contact Declan wanted. He put the phone on speaker and held it to Declan's mouth.

"Hey, baby, where are you?" came a man's voice.

"Jagger, I'm okay," Declan rasped.

There was a split-second of silence before the man said, "I'm coming, Declan. Where are you?"

"Baby, I'm okay, I swear it. Call Ronan – he'll know where they're taking me, and have Dom drive you and Ren, do you hear me? I don't want you guys driving while you're upset. Do it for me."

The man – Jagger – let out a breath and said, "Don't you fucking die on us, do you hear me, Detective?"

I saw a small smile grace Declan's pained mouth and I had to wonder if it was because of the "Detective" comment.

"It's Captain, asshole," Declan managed to say.

I swore I heard Jagger chuckle, but his voice cracked when he said, "We'll see you soon, okay, baby?"

"Yes, you will."

Elliot had tears in his eyes when he hung up the phone for Declan, and I had to wonder how much of them were for the intimate moment he'd just been witness to and how much were for the similar call his own father hadn't been able to make twenty-five years earlier.

I saw Sam hand Ryan to Elliot and then he was covering Declan's hand with his own. "Thank you," he whispered brokenly, and then he was wiping at his own wet eyes. "Thank you for saving my boy, Declan."

"I'm sorry, Sam. I should've been there. I should've been stronger. I should've been the cop he thought I was."

I heard Sam make a strangled sound. "You are, Declan. You saved his son's life without any thought to your own. You're exactly the kind of cop he knew you'd be and wherever he is, I know he's proud of you."

Declan let out a little gasp, but before he could say anything, Sam said, "Just rest, Declan. Just rest."

My eyes met Elliot's as he whispered soothing words to his brother, but I couldn't see anything beyond the fear and pain and I had no idea what that meant for us.

If there even still was an us.

~

The chaos that followed was predictable, but all that really mattered was the knowledge that Declan would be okay. Ronan had been waiting at the hospital when paramedics had arrived with him and he'd called me as soon as he'd had a chance to examine the wounded cop. The shoulder wound wasn't life-threatening and he'd likely spend the night in the hospital to be monitored for a possible concussion, but he'd already been reunited with his husbands and several other family members.

After a second set of paramedics had treated the gash on my arm where the bullet had grazed me, I refused the offer to be taken to the hospital so I could stay behind at the house to deal with the cops in case Matias was taken in for questioning. But Declan had managed to call his second-in-command from the ambulance and had told the man that Matias wasn't to be detained after giving his statement at the scene. Matias and Sam were still talking to the respective officers interviewing them and I couldn't help but watch my brother's reactions as he spoke. I was mainly worried about him becoming aggressive toward the officer, since it didn't take much to send his temper flaring. But to my surprise, he barely seemed to even be aware of the young cop taking his statement.

Because he couldn't take his eyes off Sam.

The older man was being questioned in the kitchen, which was directly in Matias's line of sight. The officers had allowed Sam to take

Ryan over to a neighbor's house so that he could get some rest. It turned out that the woman who lived next door was a retired nurse who often babysat for Ryan, so the little boy was comfortable in her presence. Elliot and I had already been interviewed, and I'd lost track of him once he'd gone to Ryan's room to pack some stuff for his brother for the night.

My emotions were all over the place as I tried to figure out how to convince Elliot I hadn't lied to him beyond what I did for a living, and that he'd stopped being a job the instant he'd said my name at that Halloween party. But I knew it wouldn't be that easy. He'd taken a big risk in trusting me with the things he had and every second I'd kept the truth from him, I'd been betraying that trust. It didn't matter that my motive hadn't been a malicious one.

"Thank you, Officer," I heard Sam say, and I watched him shake the young woman's hand before she left him in the kitchen. I knew the man was around the fifty-year-old mark, but he didn't really look it. He was well-built with dark brown hair that had very little silver in it. When I'd first met him, I'd immediately noticed the thing Elliot had been hinting at… that missing spark in his eyes. It'd definitely been there for both of his sons, but in moments like these where he got lost in himself, I had no doubt he was remembering the one part of his life that was missing and always would be.

I wouldn't have understood that before meeting Elliot. I knew it was too early to say I loved Elliot, but in my heart, I knew it was true. There was just no other explanation for what I was feeling. And I knew if I'd lost him tonight, I would have had eyes like Sam's. Even if I wasn't able to be a part of Elliot's life going forward, knowing he was still alive, still living, would be enough to keep me going. And having that flicker of hope that I could someday be with him again would have to be enough to sustain me.

It broke my heart that Sam no longer had that.

Sam seemed to sense that I was looking at him, because he looked directly at me and nodded. I knew it would probably be a while before the man trusted me if I did somehow manage to convince his son to give me a second chance, but I'd kill myself trying if the opportunity presented itself.

The older man straightened and began to head for the front door, presumably to go next door to check on Ryan, but stopped short when he encountered my brother, who was still unabashedly watching him. I had no clue how to classify the expression on Matias's face, but it was definitely throwing Sam off. The two stared at each other for a long time before Sam finally said, "Thank you."

I knew he was thanking Matias for saving Ryan's life, because there was no doubt that Blake would have shot the boy during his rampage. Matias didn't say anything at all. He just held Sam's gaze until the older man seemed to grow flustered and fled the room. It wasn't until he was gone that Matias began to get antsy. The cop noticed the switch and seemed to rush through the last of his questions. I wanted to laugh because Matias had that effect on a lot of people these days. The past thirty minutes was the longest I'd seen him sit still in a while.

The idea that it was because of some weird fascination he had with Elliot's father was just strange, so I couldn't go there. But I had to admit, it had been nice to get a glimpse of my old brother.

Matias came over to me and said, "You'll be okay?"

I nodded. Even if he hadn't liked how I'd handled the relationship with Elliot, I knew it was hard for him to see me hurting. "Thanks for having good timing, big brother," I said.

Matias smiled, though it didn't exactly reach his eyes.

"He's special, huh?" he asked.

"Yeah, he is."

He didn't respond to that, merely nodded and turned away. I saw him glance around the house once more, then he was gone. I waited for a few more minutes in the hopes that Elliot might come back, but when he didn't, I said my goodbyes to the police and texted Memphis to let him know I was leaving the scene.

It wasn't until I was halfway down the walkway that I noticed him. He was leaning against the side of my car.

I ended up slowing my step, because as eager as I'd been for this moment only minutes ago, now I was dreading it. From the way his arms were crossed and his jaw was set into a firm line, I knew he wasn't going to say anything I wanted to hear.

"Have you been out here long?" I asked when I reached him. I wanted so badly to take him in my arms, but like before the shooting, he had his arms wrapped protectively around his waist.

He shook his head. "Couldn't go back in just yet," he said as he nodded at the house. "Are you okay?" he asked as his eyes fell to the bandage on my arm.

"Barely a scratch. How's Ryan?"

"Better. He and my dad are fighting over how much candy he's allowed to eat tonight. They'll be spending the night at Mrs. Crandle's."

"And your dad?"

"Spooked. Really spooked."

Despite my good intentions to give him the space he so clearly wanted, I ended up stepping closer, crowding him back against the car. But I shoved my hands into my pockets to keep from reaching for him. "It was too close," I murmured. "Way too close."

"You should have told me, Cruz," Elliot whispered in a pained voice. "At least we might have had a chance."

Pain lanced through me at confirmation of what I already knew. He made a move to step past me, so I grabbed his arm and gently forced him back against the car. I caged him in with my arms, but I refrained from touching him since I was afraid I wouldn't be able to let him go if I did.

"Yes, I knew some stuff about you going into this thing, but the only thing I lied about was my job, because it's not exactly conducive to a first date to tell the guy you're really hoping will go out on a second date with you that you're basically a hired gun. And that's what last night was, El. A date. An incredibly sweet, fun, perfect date that I never wanted to end. You gave me your trust last night, but I gave you something too. You just didn't know it."

"What?" he asked softly.

"Me. All of me. The parts I'm afraid to show others, the parts I'm ashamed to admit to, the parts that I'm proud of. I don't have to pretend to be anything other than who I am with you. I don't have to worry about sharing my fear that my brother is going to go off the deep end someday because of what happened to me. I don't have to obsess over you thinking I was weak for not seeing that attack coming and not being able to stop it once it started. I don't have to wonder if you'll be the next person who's going to betray me. You make me feel strong and needed and so fucking... whole."

I leaned down to settle my mouth next to his ear and said, "You're not a freak, Elliot. You're fucking amazing and I would have been a lucky son of a bitch to have had the chance to love you."

He let out a little gasp. I forced myself to pull back from him, but when I went to turn away, he grabbed the sleeve of my uninjured arm hard, bunching the material between his tight fingers.

"I don't care what I am, Cruz," he murmured as soon as his eyes met mine. "As long as I can still be yours."

My heart beat painfully in my chest as I absorbed his words. He couldn't be...

"El," I whispered in disbelief.

He pushed into my arms and brushed his mouth over mine. "Take me home, Cruz. You owe me a second date."

EPILOGUE

Elliot

THREE WEEKS LATER

"*T*ell me again what it is you aren't going to do," Cruz murmured as his hand trailed down my naked back. I was covered in sweat and shaking like a leaf, but I somehow still managed to answer him.

"Come," I gasped, just as I felt the blunt head of the dildo begin to breach me.

Even though it was the first time Cruz was using the toy on me, it wasn't the first time I'd been so close to riding the edge of orgasming and not being allowed to take my pleasure. It was something Cruz liked to torture me with often, especially when the noise in my head got particularly loud.

And today it was practically screaming at me.

So I wasn't at all surprised that Cruz had spent the better part of an hour blowing, finger-fucking and rimming me until I was calling him every name in the book in the hopes he'd get frustrated and fuck me hard and fast. But the man had nerves of steel.

Something I was actually *very* grateful for, since I hadn't even once given thought to what I needed to do tomorrow. I'd been stressing about it for nearly two weeks, and while Cruz had tried to reassure me that my dad wouldn't be angry with me when I told him I had no desire to keep running the investment firm, I'd still only been able to see the decision as me somehow failing both of my fathers. Cruz had done his best to keep me on an even keel as I'd waffled back and forth on the decision and when he wasn't drugging me with mind-numbing sex, he was listening to my every worry and fear and letting me talk it out to my heart's content. And when it came to other topics that I was still trying to navigate my way through, like the peace I was trying to make in my heart with Declan Barretti, he listened, but he never urged me in one direction or the other.

But Cruz clearly had something special planned for today, because the dildo was a new development. It wasn't very big, certainly nowhere near as big as Cruz, but when he'd shown it to me, I hadn't missed the fact that it had a vibrating bullet in the tip.

I managed to follow Cruz's instructions and luxuriated in his praise as he pushed the well-lubed dildo in and out of me a few times until it was finally seated all the way inside of me. But the second he turned the thing on, all his commands flew out the window and I began humping the pillow he'd pushed under my hips to lift my ass in the air. His big hand landed heavily on my ass and then he was pressed against my back, his hips pushing the dildo deeper into me.

"Did you forget something, baby?" he asked, his voice like silk.

"Too good," I ground out.

"You know what this means," he said as he reached his hand between us and began to pull the dildo out.

No fucking way. I wouldn't survive it if he started the whole process over yet again.

"No, Cruz, I'll do better," I vowed as I turned my head. He gave me what I wanted and kissed me hard and fast. Then his lips gentled.

"You should see how beautiful you look, El," he murmured against the shell of my ear. "But you know what, my beautiful boy?"

"Wh... what?" I managed to rasp.

"That gorgeous ass still looks too empty."

I groaned as his words sank in. There was no way he was talking about...

Cruz chose that moment to up the vibration on the dildo and began thrusting his hips against mine. He reared back and grabbed both my globes with his hands and used his dick to pump the dildo deeper into me. The orgasm began to build in my balls and I knew I wouldn't be able to stop it, but before I could say anything, Cruz released me and turned off the vibration. My body collapsed in a heap on the bed and it was all I could do to keep dragging in enough oxygen to keep from passing out. I heard the snick of the cap on the lube and knew what was coming next.

I craved it, even as I feared it a little.

But my trust in Cruz was absolute. It hadn't wavered even once in the weeks since he'd admitted I gave him so many of the very things he gave me.

While our sex life was off-the-charts crazy and alternated between rough quickies in the shower or on my kitchen table to long, drawn-out encounters like the one tonight to slow, sensual lovemaking that took my breath away every time, our actual "dating life" couldn't have been more low-key. It turned out that Cruz was a homebody like me and, more often than not, we sat in front of the television playing Assassin's Creed, binge-watching shows on Netflix, or losing ourselves in cheesy B-rated horror movies that had us laughing out loud more than anything else. We'd spent nearly every single night together, usually at my place only because it was closer to my work, and when he wasn't working a case, it wasn't unusual for him to meet me for lunch.

It turned out Cruz's breakfast-for-dinner obsession applied to lunch too.

All in all, our compatibility sometimes scared me because it was almost too easy. I often found myself waiting for the other shoe to drop, but Cruz kept reassuring me that even if it did, he wasn't going anywhere.

And I believed him.

Cruz's hand palmed my ass in a gentle caress. "Whose ass is this, baby?" he murmured.

"Yours," I said without hesitation. "Only yours, Cruz."

Cruz's hands closed around my hips so he could draw me up so that I was on all fours. I groaned when the vibration on the dildo started up again, but the few minutes he'd given me as he'd prepared himself had allowed my body to come down a couple of notches. But I knew it wouldn't take much to send me right back to that precipice he'd had me hanging off all night.

I felt a slight tug on the dildo as Cruz got situated behind me, then his hand came down to rest in the middle of my back. "Breathe out, baby," he said gently. I eagerly did as he said, even as tension racked my body. A split-second of nothingness passed, then I felt it.

Cruz's crown pushing against my entrance.

Right beneath the dildo.

"Oh God," I gasped when his dick pierced my body. The pressure was almost too much, which meant it was just about fucking perfect. My head spun as my body lit up. The pain turned into the familiar burn, but it lasted only seconds because Cruz pushed another inch of himself into me. I gasped and reached behind me to grab his thigh. I could feel his muscles flexing and realized I wasn't the only one dealing with the strain.

Cruz didn't ask me if I wanted to stop or if I wanted more.

Because he knew.

Just like all the other times that he instinctively knew what I needed. Sometimes before I did. The shame I'd felt that first night was nonexistent for me now and I refused to try and label what Cruz and I did with one another. I wasn't his slave and he wasn't my master. But I wasn't just his lover, either. We were so many things to each other and trying to simplify it with a label wasn't necessary or warranted.

"Halfway, baby."

Sweat was dripping off my forehead. I would have guessed that he was all the way in, considering how full I felt. My lungs burned as I tried to breathe through the lingering pain. The good thing was that my dick had softened somewhat, so I wasn't in any immediate danger of disobeying Cruz's rule not to come.

I had no clue how much time passed before Cruz's balls brushed against mine. His fingers were biting into my hips hard enough that I'd have bruises in the morning, a fact I was very, very pleased about.

"Fuck, so tight," Cruz muttered. His hands caressed my back as he held there for a moment, then they disappeared. I let out a hoarse shout when Cruz's dick and the dildo pulled out of me in one slow, fluid motion.

When he shoved back inside me, I dropped my shoulders to the bed, because my elbows wouldn't hold my weight anymore. "Cruz," I whimpered.

"Just a little more, baby. It's gonna feel so good when I send you flying."

I might have nodded, I wasn't sure. I wasn't sure of anything except for how alive my body felt. Like my entire central nervous system had migrated south and was tied to Cruz's cock.

Fast.

Slow.

Hard.

Soft.

Didn't matter how he fucked me – every single way was heaven. My orgasm began building in my balls.

"Can't stop it," I managed to whisper.

Part of me was actually heartbroken that I wouldn't be able to hold out any longer, because I wanted to please Cruz by following his rules, but I shouldn't have even worried about it because he leaned over my back and said, "Don't fight it, baby. Come for me. Just me."

In one fluid movement, Cruz pulled his dick and the dildo out and then it was just his dick shuttling in and out of me. He didn't bother going for my cock, probably because he knew I didn't need his touch there. His weight pushed me completely down on the bed and he wrapped his arms around my chest. His lips pressed against my neck and then he was peppering my skin with gentle kisses.

It was in complete contrast to how hard he was fucking me.

I feared the orgasm that was overtaking me. It just kept building and building and every time I was sure I would go over the edge, I didn't. When I whispered Cruz's name with a measure of uncertainty, he was right there to remind me that he had me and that I was safe to let go. So that's what I did. I stopped worrying about when I would fly, or if I even would. It didn't matter. It had never been about the orgasm, anyway. It had been about that moment where I could give myself over to someone else and trust them with my safekeeping. It was letting go of the noise in my head and the fear of not being good enough and accepting that those things didn't matter – they didn't define me.

I was still the same Elliot I'd always been.

I was just okay with it now.

I was able to see that the man I'd become was perfect in his imperfections. He was brave despite his fear. He was allowed to fail, even though he rarely did. And he was worth loving, even when it was sometimes hard to love himself.

"El, are you still with me, baby?" Cruz asked.

I nodded. "Always with you," I managed to get out.

"Do you love me, El?"

There was no hesitation as I said, "More than anything."

The pressure in my balls finally exploded, but not before Cruz gave me the last thing I'd ever need. "Do you know how much I love you?"

I didn't answer him as the orgasm washed over me in wave after violent wave, or even when I felt his release begin to burn my insides. It wasn't until our breathing returned to normal and Cruz pulled out of me so he could turn me over and cradle me in his arms that I finally responded.

"The perfect amount, Cruz. You love me the perfect amount."

He smiled and held my gaze for a long time before he gently kissed me and then settled his head on my chest so he could listen to my heartbeat. He was silent as he held me that way, but I didn't mind because just like everything else he'd done for me tonight and every other that had come before it, it was exactly what I needed.

And it was absolutely perfect.

The End

ABOUT THE AUTHOR

Dear Reader,

I hope you enjoyed Cruz and Elliot's story. And yes, Matias and Sam will be getting their own book as part of *The Protectors* series at some point!

As an independent author, I am always grateful for feedback so if you have the time and desire, please leave a review, good or bad, so I can continue to find out what my readers like and don't like. You can also send me feedback via email at sloane@sloanekennedy.com

Join my Facebook Fan Group: Sloane's Secret Sinners

Connect with me:
www.sloanekennedy.com
sloane@sloanekennedy.com

SERIES READING ORDER

All of my series cross over with one another so I've provided a couple of recommended reading orders for you. If you want to start with the Protectors books, use the first list. If you want to follow the books according to timing, use the second list. Note that you can skip any of the books (including M/F) as each was written to be a standalone story.

Note that some books may not be readily available on all retail sites

Recommended Reading Order (Use this list if you want to start with "The Protectors" series)
1. Absolution (m/m/m) (The Protectors, #1)
2. Salvation (m/m) (The Protectors, #2)
3. Retribution (m/m) (The Protectors, #3)
4. Gabriel's Rule (m/f) (The Escort Series, #1)
5. Shane's Fall (m/f) (The Escort Series, #2)
6. Logan's Need (m/m) (The Escort Series, #3)
7. Finding Home (m/m/m) (Finding Series, #1)
8. Finding Trust (m/m) (Finding Series, #2)
9. Loving Vin (m/f) (Barretti Security Series, #1)

10. Redeeming Rafe (m/m) (Barretti Security Series, #2)
11. Saving Ren (m/m/m) (Barretti Security Series, #3)
12. Freeing Zane (m/m) (Barretti Security Series, #4)
13. Finding Peace (m/m) (Finding Series, #3)
14. Finding Forgiveness (m/m) (Finding Series, #4)
15. Forsaken (m/m) (The Protectors, #4)
16. Vengeance (m/m/m) (The Protectors, #5)
17. A Protectors Family Christmas (The Protectors, #5.5)
18. Atonement (m/m) (The Protectors, #6)
19. Revelation (m/m) (The Protectors, #7)
20. Redemption (m/m) (The Protectors, #8)
21. Finding Hope (m/m/m) (Finding Series, #5)
22. Defiance (m/m) (The Protectors, #9)
23. Protecting Elliot: A Protectors Novella (m/m)

Recommended Reading Order (Use this list if you want to follow according to timing)

1. Gabriel's Rule (m/f) (The Escort Series, #1)
2. Shane's Fall (m/f) (The Escort Series, #2)
3. Logan's Need (m/m) (The Escort Series, #3)
4. Finding Home (m/m/m) (Finding Series, #1)
5. Finding Trust (m/m) (Finding Series, #2)
6. Loving Vin (m/f) (Barretti Security Series, #1)
7. Redeeming Rafe (m/m) (Barretti Security Series, #2)
8. Saving Ren (m/m/m) (Barretti Security Series, #3)
9. Freeing Zane (m/m) (Barretti Security Series, #4)
10. Finding Peace (m/m) (Finding Series, #3)
11. Finding Forgiveness (m/m) (Finding Series, #4)
12. Absolution (m/m/m) (The Protectors, #1)
13. Salvation (m/m) (The Protectors, #2)
14. Retribution (m/m) (The Protectors, #3)
15. Forsaken (m/m) (The Protectors, #4)
16. Vengeance (m/m/m) (The Protectors, #5)
17. A Protectors Family Christmas (The Protectors, #5.5)
18. Atonement (m/m) (The Protectors, #6)

19. Revelation (m/m) (The Protectors, #7)
20. Redemption (m/m) (The Protectors, #8)
21. Finding Hope (m/m/m) (Finding Series, #5)
22. Defiance (m/m) (The Protectors, #9)
23. Protecting Elliot: A Protectors Novella (m/m)

SERIES CROSSOVER CHART

Protectors/Barrettis/Finding Crossover Chart

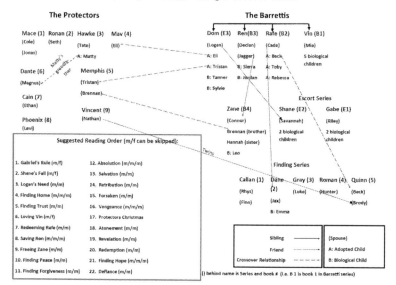

The Protectors

Mace (1) Ronan (2) Hawke (3) Mav (4)
{Cole}   {Seth}   {Tate}   {Eli}
{Jonas}

                      A: Matty

Dante (6)   Memphis (5)
{Magnus}   {Tristan}
                     {Brennan}

Cain (7)
{Ethan}

                     Vincent (9)
Phoenix (8)   {Nathan}
{Levi}

The Barrettis

Dom (E3)   Ren(B3)   Rafe (B2)   Vin (B1)
{Logan}   {Declan} {Cade}   {Mia}
A: Eli   {Jagger} A: Beck   5 biological
A: Tristan B: Sierra A: Toby   children
B: Tanner B: Jordan A: Rebecca
B: Sylvie

                              Escort Series

Zane (B4)   Shane (E2)   Gabe (E1)
{Connor}   {Savannah}   {Riley}
Brennan (brother) 2 biological   2 biological
Hannah (sister)   children   children
B: Leo

                   Finding Series

Callan (1) Dane   Gray (3) Roman (4) Quinn (5)
{Rhys}   (2)   {Luke}   {Hunter}   {Beck}
{Finn}   {Jax}   {Brody}
            B: Emma

Suggested Reading Order (m/f can be skipped):

1. Gabriel's Rule (m/f)
2. Shane's Fall (m/f)
3. Logan's Need (m/m/m)
4. Finding Home (m/m/m)
5. Finding Trust (m/m)
6. Loving Vin (m/f)
7. Redeeming Rafe (m/m)
8. Saving Ren (m/m/m)
9. Freeing Zane (m/m)
10. Finding Peace (m/m)
11. Finding Forgiveness (m/m)
12. Absolution (m/m/m)
13. Salvation (m/m)
14. Retribution (m/m)
15. Forsaken (m/m)
16. Vengeance (m/m/m)
17. Protectors Christmas
18. Atonement (m/m)
19. Revelation (m/m)
20. Redemption (m/m)
21. Finding Hope (m/m/m)
22. Defiance (m/m)

Sibling	————————	{Spouse}
Friend	··················	A: Adopted Child
Crossover Relationship	– – – – – –	B: Biological Child

() behind name is Series and book # (i.e. B 1 is book 1 in Barretti series)

ALSO BY SLOANE KENNEDY

(Note: Not all titles will be available on all retail sites)

Pelican Bay Series

Locked in Silence (M/M)

The Escort Series

Gabriel's Rule (M/F)

Shane's Fall (M/F)

Logan's Need (M/M)

Barretti Security Series

Loving Vin (M/F)

Redeeming Rafe (M/M)

Saving Ren (M/M/M)

Freeing Zane (M/M)

Finding Series

Finding Home (M/M/M)

Finding Trust (M/M)

Finding Peace (M/M)

Finding Forgiveness (M/M)

Finding Hope (M/M/M)

The Protectors

Absolution (M/M/M)

Salvation (M/M)

Retribution (M/M)

Forsaken (M/M)

Vengeance (M/M/M)

A Protectors Family Christmas

Atonement (M/M)

Revelation (M/M)

Redemption (M/M)

Defiance (M/M)

Protecting Elliot (M/M)

Non-Series

Letting Go (M/F)

54472542R00064

Made in the USA
San Bernardino, CA
17 October 2017